My Life
as a
Diamond

My Life
as a
Diamond

JENNY
MANZER

ORCA BOOK PUBLISHERS

Library and Archives Canada Cataloguing in Publication

Manzer, Jenny, author
My life as a diamond / Jenny Manzer.

Issued in print and electronic formats.
ISBN 978-1-4598-1831-6 (softcover).—ISBN 978-1-4598-1832-3 (PDF).—
ISBN 978-1-4598-1833-0 (EPUB)

I. Title.
PS8626.A6927M9 2018   jC813'.6   C2017-907670-1
C2017-907671-X

First published in the United States, 2018
Library of Congress Control Number: 2018933731

Summary: Talented baseball player Caspar Cadman has a great arm and a big secret. He used to live life as a girl called Cassandra.

Orca Book Publishers is dedicated to preserving the environment and has printed this book on Forest Stewardship Council® certified paper.

Orca Book Publishers gratefully acknowledges the support for its publishing programs provided by the following agencies: the Government of Canada through the Canada Book Fund and the Canada Council for the Arts, and the Province of British Columbia through the BC Arts Council and the Book Publishing Tax Credit.

Edited by Tanya Trafford
Cover design by Julie McLaughlin and Teresa Bubela
Cover artwork by Julie McLaughlin
Author photo by Helene Cyr

ORCA BOOK PUBLISHERS
orcabook.com

Printed and bound in Canada.

21 20 19 18 • 4 3 2 1

*For my sister, Patricia Kathryn Manzer (1967–2017),
beloved aunt and dedicated reader.*

*And for all the kids like Caz, who are brave enough
to be their true selves.*

See you at the ballpark.

*Every strike brings me closer
to the next home run.*
—George Herman "Babe" Ruth Jr.

*If everyone had to be perfect all the time,
nothing would ever get done.*
—Coach Vij

It all started with a haircut. A week before my tenth birthday, I came from home from school and told my mom I wanted my hair to be cut—like, *now*. My hair suddenly felt like this heavy, weighted thing, not right on my head at all. I always wore it in a single braid, and it kept thump-thumping me on the back when I ran, like someone tapping me on the shoulder.

"You have baseball practice," my mom said. I always had baseball practice. I was on two base-ball teams—one for regular kids and the other for players who were really good. I don't mean to brag, but it's the truth. Even when I was five years old, I could throw a ball almost to the end of our street.

"We can make time," I said. "It won't take long."

She must have known by my tone that I was serious, because she agreed, and we drove to The Chop Shop at the mall. My hands were trembling a little bit, the way they did when I practiced pitching and lost track of time. But some days you just know something.

The Chop Shop was one of those cheapo hair places, but it had special seats for kids—red race cars for boys and a splashy pink for girls.

"Hi, Cassandra," said Elena. She had been cutting my hair since I was three. There is a photo in our family album of me having my first real haircut with her. She's dabbing my nose with a big brush that sweeps away the hair, and I am laughing.

This day, though, I was not laughing. I sat down in one of the regular black chairs for adults before she could ask which kids' seat I wanted.

"Just here for a trim?" she asked, taking out the elastic band from my braid. She raked her fingers through my long brown hair. The salon smelled of the citrus shampoo I usually enjoy having lathered into my hair. But there was no time for that. I remember thinking, This is it.

"No," I said. "I'd like to cut it all off."

"Oh," she said. "Short and sassy? Like *short hair, don't care*?" she asked, glancing at my mom in the mirror.

Short hair, don't care was what all the celebrities tweeted when they chopped off their hair. Even I knew that. My mom held her purse in front of her chest. She looked as if she were preparing to be hit by a wild pitch.

"I do care. I want it short," I said and crossed my arms. I was already wearing my baseball uniform. Red and white. Number 3—my lucky number.

"Okay, you're the boss. I'll just take a few inches off to start, in case you change your mind," said Elena.

I heard the scissors slowly close over a chunk of my hair, and the first piece fell to the floor. Elena started working faster then, whistling under her breath, her fingers deft with the scissors.

"Still good?" asked Elena, stopping to look at me in the mirror. She smiled. She had round cheeks with lots of pink rouge, and shiny red-blond hair that she sometimes wore curly and sometimes wore flat, as if she'd ironed it. I'd always liked Elena. She often wanted details about my latest baseball game.

"Keep cutting, please," I said.

My mom's eyes got bigger as more and more of my hair covered the floor tiles. The growing pile reminded me of the grass trimmings left behind after my parents cut the lawn.

"Cassie, are you sure?" Elena asked. "Mrs. Cadman, is this okay?"

I was *so* sure. I was like Mike Trout soaring up in the outfield to make one of those amazing airborne catches and stop a home run. It was time to do something. Take a jump.

I guess I'd never thought about the other player, the one denied the run. The one who shuffles back to the dugout. The one who is disappointed because they imagined it would turn out differently. I hadn't thought about my mom.

"Well, it's her hair," said my mom in a tiny voice, like she couldn't get enough air.

When Elena was done I ran my hand over my hair. It was cut to just below my ears, but not buzzed or spiky, so it felt smooth and cool. I ran my fingers along the bare skin on the back of my neck. My head felt light and free. My mom picked up a piece of my hair from the salon floor and tucked it into her purse. Our eyes met in the mirror, but we didn't say anything. She went over to the counter where Elena was ringing up the cost of the haircut. Elena was singing along under her breath to the pop music piped in, cheerful as ever, like it was no big deal that I'd just had all my hair shorn off. Lots of ball players wear their hair long, flowing down past their helmets. A few have bald or shaved heads, like Albert Pujols or Adrián Beltré. But they all have their own style. Now I had mine.

In the car on the way to practice, I knew I had something else to say.

"Mom," I said, "I'd like you to call me Caz, like my baseball nickname."

"Cassie, this has gone far enough. You're my daughter, and I named you Cassandra. Your friends can call you Caz, but I'll call you Cassie."

"Cassie is a girl's name, Mom. I don't want a girl's name."

My mom darted into a spot at the ballpark, crookedly, her hands gripping the steering wheel. She cranked up the parking brake.

"Cassie, you *are* a girl." She stared at me, looking confused, as if fog were steaming a window between us and she couldn't quite see me. My mom has soft brown eyes and shoulder-length hair the same shade as mine. She wears one little swipe of lipstick, and that's it.

"Mom," I said, my breath heaving out and making a whooshing sound like a fastball past your ear. "I don't think I *am* a girl."

And not long after that almost everything changed. I decided my new full name would be Caspar. My dad got a new job flying planes for an American company. We moved from our house in Toronto all the way to Washington State, a place with lots of rain and hardly any snow. I left my own baseball team, the Leslieville Lightning. I left my favorite major league team, the Toronto Blue Jays. My dad let me see one last game at Rogers Centre, and I cried when the players came out—and even for ACE, the Blue Jays' mascot, with his number 00.

That was what happened to me when we moved. My dial was set back to 00. We went thousands of miles away, where nobody knew us. And only my mom, my dad, my dog and I knew I had ever been called Cassandra.

The Tryout

There were things I missed about home. I missed my best friend, Matt. I missed some of the boys on my house-league team, the Lightning—but not all of them. Definitely not all of them. I missed the ballpark where I'd played since I was four, starting with T-ball. I moved on to baseball when I was five, joining a group of seven-year-olds. I'd worked my way up to play on the Red Devils, an all-star team. They named a hot dog ("The Devil Dog") at my local ballpark after the Red Devils, because we were *that* good. I was the only girl on the team, but everyone was cool with it because of my arm. *That girl's got some arm*, they always said. The hot dog was epic. There was nothing better than eating one after winning a game. So there were good memories, as well as the bad. We moved to our new house in Redburn at the end of June, just after school ended, *making a clean break*, my mom said.

"Mom," I said. "There's nothing to *doooo*." She was busy unwrapping dishes, all that stuff we didn't use a lot, like the fancy bowls and plates my parents got as wedding presents.

"You can help me unpack."

"That's boring."

"Yes, it is, Caz," she agreed, frowning. My dad was working. At least he just did short little hops, not overnight flights. He'd be home for dinner.

She seemed to be getting used to my new name. Back home we'd gone to see a therapist named Miss Linda. We'd talked all about "comfort zones" and "next steps." I had always preferred to wear Adidas pants and hoodies and board shorts, and so I'd officially packed away the sundresses and barrettes for good. Mom had helped me stuff everything into a giant garbage bag, and then we'd dropped it off at the Salvation Army. Sometimes people have to do brave things.

Summers were cooler in Washington State than at home in Ontario. I was also still getting used to the green money. I worried that one day I would accidentally give someone twenty bucks for a bag of chips.

The weather was cool, and it was spitting rain. The TV newscasters were calling it "Junuary." I looked up the forecasts on the Internet, and at home it was nothing but sunbursts. But I didn't really want to go back, not after what had happened.

I trudged downstairs to our rec room. My dad had promised he'd get us a Ping-Pong table for the new house, and a foosball table too. I could invite my friends over, he said. If I ever made any friends. I turned on the TV to watch a DVD of the Blue Jays in the playoffs and plunked myself onto the couch, pulling my cap down on my head and folding my arms over my chest. What was the point of anything without baseball?

"Caspar, no," my mom called from the kitchen.

"No, what?" I asked. She was probably going to tell me to get outside. We'd been in Redburn for five days. I'd stayed inside almost the whole time, like some strange person on one of those reality TV shows.

"No more TV. Out," she said. "Take J.R. for a walk. Go find the park. It's close, and it's got a ball diamond. I can't believe you haven't checked it out yet."

J.R. eyed me. He looked kind of sad himself, the way golden retrievers can. He was no longer a puppy, even though he acted like it. The initials were short for Jackie Robinson, the great baseball player. My dad had told me all about him. J.R. seemed confused that we had moved. I guess all the smells were different.

"You want go out, buddy?"

He did. He trotted to the front door, his fluffy tail dusting the furniture as he went.

"Caz," my mom said as she poured herself, like, her eighteenth cup of coffee. "If you meet people in the neighborhood, say hello."

"I will, I will," I muttered. J.R. looked so happy to go out that I nearly felt happy too. I'd be just another boy in the neighborhood. A boy with a secret. But maybe all boys had secrets.

The rain had let up a bit, and sun tried to burn through the gray beard of clouds. Redburn was a suburb of SeaTac, which was a suburb of Seattle. We were in a sub-suburb. We'd moved here because Redburn was a small, friendly place, my mom said, close to my dad's job at the airport. Wikipedia had told me that Redburn has a population of sixteen thousand. It said nothing about baseball teams.

J.R. and I walked for a couple of blocks, past all the parked minivans and lawns as green as billiard tables, and I watched my sneakers move forward. When we lived in Toronto, I never spent much time at home—or alone—because I was usually at practice or at school. Since I had no friends to play catch with in Redburn, I'd been throwing a baseball against my rebounder net, over and over. It helped settle my busy brain.

J.R. and I headed to the local park, following my mom's instructions. J.R. acted like he was a puppy again, bouncing along and smelling the flowering bushes. We'd had J.R. for most of my life. My mom used to have a framed photo of me from kindergarten on her dresser. I was wearing a pink dress, my arms wrapped around J.R., who was about a year old. That might have been the last time I wore pink—or a dress, for that matter. Not without a fight anyway. When we unpacked in Redburn, I asked her to put the picture away. I didn't want to see old photos from before.

I sat down on a bench, regretting that I hadn't brought my glove. My hand felt bare without it. I wished my dad would come home to play with me. I stood up to boot a baguette lying on the ground out of the reach of J.R., who would have downed it in a second. He was getting a bit chunky, Mom said. Someone must have dropped it when they were having a picnic, because the trash can was full of paper plates and empty wrappers.

J.R. sniffed around the bench while I stared at the empty ball diamond. Someone had weeded it. It was ready to go. I wondered when summer ball started. Tryouts were already under way back home in Toronto.

"You play?" I heard a voice say. The voice belonged to a boy. He looked about my age, but he was a bit shorter. He had a sprinkling of freckles on his nose and wore a navy-and-teal Seattle Mariners cap.

I felt my Jays cap. I owned two, but today I was wearing my favorite—it had mesh at the back to keep your head cool. Not that you needed it in this kind of summer weather.

"Yeah, I play," I said. Oh, I was supposed to say hello, I remembered. I couldn't tell if he was nice or not. I wished people just came with signs that told you whether they were friend or foe, because I really needed a friend.

"I'm Hank Ottenburg." Then he kind of fake coughed into his hand while muttering something.

"What?"

"You heard me. I'm the best hitter there is around here."

"*Re-ally*?" I asked. "And what position do you play?"

"I do it all, but I'm known as a hitter. Actually, I'm known as The Hitman."

"Hank the Hitman." I tested it out, trying not to laugh. The last thing I needed was to earn an enemy my first day out. I had a definite feeling Hank was making things up as he went along.

"You can call me Slugger," he said.

"I think I'll call you Hank," I said. "I'm Caspar Cadman. You can call me Caz. You know, like Yaz." Yaz was the nickname of Carl Yastrzemski. When you're as good as Yaz, you become the answer to a trivia question. Answer: Legendary left fielder for Boston Red Sox. Aka "Captain Carl." Greatness personified.

"Caz, hand me that baguette." Hank squinted, even though the sun was thin and lemonade pale.

"You hungry?" I asked. I wasn't sure about Hank yet. Poor J.R. thought I was going to throw the bread for him, like a stick. A string of drool streamed out the side of his mouth.

"Just do it," Hank said.

"That sounds familiar," I said, but Hank didn't laugh. I tossed him the baguette, which was now coated with dirt. Who brings a baguette to a ballpark anyway? Ballparks are for hot dogs. What kind of place was this?

"Now throw a rock at me," said Hank, holding the baguette like a bat.

"What?"

"Not at me, but like a pitch."

I picked up a smooth stone from the ground and lobbed it underhand at Hank. He swung at it, lips pursed in concentration. He missed it. He wasn't even close. J.R.'s ears perked up, his shiny eyes fixed on the bread.

"See that?" Hank said.

"See what? You missed it."

"But my cut, man, my swing."

"Maybe they should call you Swinger Hank then," I suggested. This kid was weird, going all braggy-pants when he really couldn't hit.

"Look," said Hank, tossing the bread into the wire wastebasket by the bench. He made that play at least. Maybe he was better at basketball. "I'm willing to let you be on my crew, but I need to know one thing."

I waited. Hank had a crew?

"Do you like the Texas Rangers?"

"I *detest* the Texas Rangers," I said. Nana Cadman says the key to relationships is honesty. A Texas Ranger pitcher once grabbed a Blue Jays rally towel at a Toronto game and pretended to use it to wipe his butt. Not cool. The Houston Astros were fine. Rangers, nope.

"Same," said Hank, satisfied. "We're the exact same."

"We're not," I said. "I'm a Blue Jays fan."

"That where you're from, Toronto?"

"Yep. Thereabouts."

"I could tell that you had an accent."

I did not have an accent. Or did I? What did a Canadian accent sound like?

"Listen," I said. "You can always improve your hitting. You want me to throw you a few?"

"If you're not too afraid of my heat." Hank was grinning. I guess he wanted someone to play with too.

"I think I'll be okay," I said. "Let's go to my house and get my bat and glove." It was the first time I had referred to the new place as "my house."

On the way Hank chattered away like a junior sportscaster, telling me all about the neighborhood kids and the ball clubs. He launched into a long story about this walk-off home run he had scored at the end of the regular season. I wondered if it really had been a home run he *wished* he'd scored. It was hard to tell. Tryouts for summer ball were in two days, he said. I got that part loud and clear.

~

Sometimes I thought my braid was still there on my back, and I'd feel to make sure it was gone. I liked my short hair. I felt best of all when I was in my baseball gear—long pants, baseball jersey, ballcap and cleats. I had the real deal too, baseball cleats, not the ones for soccer. The spikes on baseball cleats remind me of shark's teeth.

"You look ready to play," my dad said, smiling. He always said that having the right uniform was an important part of baseball.

He wore a baseball cap too—a battered one with the Chicago Cubs logo. I was okay with it, at least until playoff time, because the Cubs were in a different division than the Jays.

"I am," I said. Baseball was all about confidence. You had to believe you could do it, to see yourself completing a play even before it happened. Confidence without swagger. You had to keep them guessing.

The tryouts were later that day, at a bigger park a few miles outside of Redburn. Hank told me he'd be there, *ready to hit the sticks*. (His words. I think Hank swallowed a baseball dictionary and just burps this stuff out.)

Summer ball was supposed to be more relaxed, but it never really was. Everyone would be eyeing up the contenders for the spring league. I wasn't worried. This was my chance to show the other kids that I could play.

The phone rang just as we were leaving for the tryouts, which made me jump. Guess I was more nervous than I thought. I was standing in the hall, making sure I had everything packed in my baseball bag.

"Caspar, phone for you," called Mom from the living room.

"Who is it?" I felt bad thinking it, but I hoped it wasn't my grandma and grandpa Ames, my mom's parents. My grandma didn't know why I insisted on dressing like a boy when she sent me all those pretty dresses in the mail. My grandpa, a retired Navy captain, thought baseball was a good way to get some fresh air but otherwise a waste of time. We didn't visit with them very often. Now that Grandpa was retired they spent a lot of time planning cruises and doing stuff with their church.

"It's Nana," my mom said, appearing in the hallway. "She wants to talk to you."

My mom handed me the phone before heading down to the basement, where the dryer was buzzing.

"Well, hello. Is this Miss Delish?" I heard.

It was my Nana Cadman, my dad's mom. She was a smoker once and still had a raspy voice. She'd made me promise never to smoke, and I told her the only thing that would be smoking was the end of my bat, which made her laugh. I liked making her laugh. She was one of my favorite people. And she loved baseball.

"Na-*na*," I scolded. I'd asked her not to call me that anymore. She'd been calling me Miss Delish since I was tiny.

"Sorry, sorry," she said. "Old habits die hard." I could hear her rickety fan whirring in the background. My dad had asked her to move to Redburn too, but she didn't want to leave all her Toronto friends, especially her bridge group.

"That's okay, Nana." You just had to roll with Nana. We'd all learned that.

"Did you get the book I sent you?"

"Yes, I love it." It was by my bed in my new room: *The Biggest Book of Baseball*. She'd mailed it so it would be waiting for me at my new address.

"Just wanted to wish you good luck before the tryouts, sweetie." Nana sounded sad. She used to come to all my games. I still wished she would change her mind and move to Redburn. I wished Matt would too. There was only the one time he kinda let me down. I found it hard to imagine a world where he wasn't my friend.

"It's just summer ball, Nana."

"Show 'em what you're made of," she said, ignoring my words. Once Nana got on a roll, she was like someone riding a shopping cart down a hill— safest to let her finish.

"*There are only two seasons, winter and baseball,*" she continued. "Bill Veeck said that. You know who he was?"

"Mrs. Veeck's son?"

"No, smarty-pants. He was a ball-club owner. Champion of the little guy." Nana loved champions of the little guy.

"Nana, I think I'd better go. Tryouts start in half an hour."

"Okay, sunshine. Call me later and tell me how it went. Love you."

"Love you too, Nana."

After putting down the phone, I picked up one of the photo albums from the pile my mom was organizing. It read *Baby's First Year*. My mom liked to make prints of photos. She was old-fashioned that way. She rolled her own piecrusts and read real books too. She said she liked to hold things in her hands.

I opened the first page, and there was tiny, rosy-skinned me, wrapped in a flannel towel, a yellow one because they hadn't known if I would be a boy or a girl. There were photos of me with my mom, my dad, Nana and Granddad Cadman before he died of colon cancer.

There was a photo of me as a baby, wearing a bib that said *Baby's First Christmas*. Grandma Ames, my mom's mom, was holding me tucked close to her chest, and Grandpa Ames was next to her, his hand on her shoulder. He was smiling like I was the best thing invented since ice cream.

I hoped that one day they would love me again the way they had when I was a baby.

"Sure I can't stay?" asked my dad, standing by our station wagon. He still had his Cubs cap on. He'd worn it forever, through all their losing years. He squinted in the sun, which was strong and warm. Maybe summer would come to rainy Redburn after all.

"No, Dad, but thanks." Having him there would make me more nervous. It was only summer ball, but the tryouts were held at a big park with a lot of kids. It seemed airport-busy. At least I knew the people in this town took their baseball seriously.

"I'll pick you up at three," he said again. He'd said that at least four times on the ride there, past all the malls and gas stations and fast-food joints. I scanned the field. Coaches in ballcaps paced around, carrying pylons and buckets of balls. Mothers and fathers chased after little brothers and sisters. Parents and kids were already warming up, playing catch. Typical tryout.

"I'll be fine, Dad."

"Okay, Caspar," my dad said. I liked hearing him say my new name.

"Okay," I said, more to myself than anyone. I tucked in my Red Devils team jersey. I still loved it. It was thin and light and cherry red. Plus, we'd taken the crown, winning our area championships the previous year for our age group. They'd be the team to beat this summer. But I wouldn't be there to play third base.

"Go get 'em," my dad said, smiling, but behind the smile I could see a ripple of concern. My parents often looked at me that way now. I knew they were worried. Nana told me we all have our path to walk. I wished she would remind them.

As soon as my dad drove off, I felt sad. I should have told him to stay. There were lots of parents pacing around in tracksuits and yoga pants, most of them glancing at their palms every few seconds as if they were holding the key to the universe and not a smartphone.

"Ethan hit .400 in the spring season," one dad told another dad, not looking up from his phone.

I noticed one kid, super tall, striding into the parking lot. He wore black Converse high-tops instead of cleats. I watched as he stuck his arm in the open window of a black minivan and grabbed a For Sale sign from the back. He then placed it on top of a white sports car.

The boy caught me watching. He turned and scowled.

"What're you looking at?" he asked.

"Nothing," I muttered. "Just getting in the zone."

"Yeah, well, get out of my zone," he said, bumping me with his baseball bag as he passed.

Don't let them mess with you, Cadman. Steel and oak. That's what I tell myself in my head sometimes. I imagine I'm made of steel or oak inside, sturdy and strong. No room for butterflies. I saw it in a baseball video online, how you can get rid of nerves by telling yourself you are made of tough materials. The idea is that if the brain believes, the performance will follow, or something like that.

I walked up to the table of volunteers with clipboards and told them my name.

"Caspar Cadman. That's a great baseball name, honey," said the lady with all the forms. She was wearing a tennis outfit, visor and all, which made me question her commitment to baseball. "Caspar, you can start at the batting station."

"Thanks," I said, taking the number she gave me to wear. We'd be tested, given points for our various skills and then assigned to teams. I knew the drill. Baseball is baseball. It's the same all over the world, which is kind of cool. I don't speak Spanish, but I bet I could still play a game of scrub with a kid from the Dominican Republic, no problem.

"*Great baseball name, honey!*" a voice behind me said in a fake falsetto.

I walked past Converse Guy, careful not to bump him with my baseball bag even though I was tempted. *Let your game do your talking*, my dad always said.

"Kyle Budworth," Converse Guy told the volunteers at the table. He was big. It was hard to believe he was U-11.

I went to the batting station and stood in line. When it was my turn in the cage, I hit every ball that came at me, *pop*, *pop*, *pop*. When I left the cage I noticed Hank in line. I gave him a wave, still wearing my batting glove. Hank raised one hand in greeting and gave me a nervous smile. I wondered if we were friends.

First Inning

I was outside, throwing against my rebounder net, when I found out I was part of a team again. My dad wandered out to the driveway with his phone to read me the email. I was now one-tenth of the Redburn Ravens.

My new coach's name was Vijay Goel. His son was Arjun. My dad read out the rest of the team names. One was familiar—Hank Ottenburg.

"I know him," I said. *Throw, bounce, catch.* The rebounder net looked like something Spiderman would spin.

"Yeah? He any good?"

"He *thinks* he's good." Then I felt bad for saying that, because I'd liked Hank. He was goofy, but in a positive way.

"Well, I'm glad you'll have a friend."

I shrugged. We'd played catch at the park a couple of times. Hank had tried to show me how to do some grips for pitches, as if we didn't have them in Canada.

My dad and I sometimes have trouble talking since I made the change. Mostly when we hang out, we throw the ball, or he pitches to me so I can practice batting. I imagine he wishes things were different. I wish that too sometimes. But wishing things are different never works.

"First practice is tomorrow," said my dad. "I'll be working, but your mom will take you."

"Sounds good," I said, keeping my face neutral. I was nervous about practice—about how I would play and whether any of the kids would know I was different.

"Want to go to the park and hit a few before I have to go to work?"

"Sure," I said, straightening my Jays cap. I hoped the Ravens' team uniforms weren't yellow. For some reason I had this idea that yellow was bad luck.

After dinner I overheard part of a conversation I wished I hadn't. My mom was sitting on her bed, talking to her parents, Grandma and Grandpa Ames. She didn't notice me standing in the doorway. I knew there had been some discussion of them coming to visit around Canada Day, which of course was not a big deal in the U.S. of A. But July 1 had come and gone.

"Mom, Dad, if you're going to visit, you have to respect Caspar's wishes. It's his life. No dresses, no comments about his hair…No, Dad, it's the way he feels."

There was a long pause.

"When you both come on the line like this, I feel that you're ganging up on me."

Miss Linda had told us to try to express ourselves this way—"When you do *this*, I feel *that*." It was part of effective communication, she said.

My grandpa's voice got so loud I could hear it through the phone. He was probably talking about God. He credited God for helping him get through some tough times when he was in the Navy.

"Dad," she sighed. "I really need you to support me on this." My mom jammed her fingers into her hair and rubbed her scalp, as if trying to erase something in her head.

"Mom," she said, trying another route. "When Cassandra was three, she asked me to put her back in my tummy. She said something had gone wrong." Her voice caught like a shawl snagging on a nail.

My mom stopped. Grandpa was probably interrupting. He always interrupted. My mom told me that when she was a kid he'd return home from being out at sea and act like life hadn't gone on while he was away. As if the whole world had stopped until he came back.

"We'd rather have a happy boy than a miserable girl," my mom said. I could tell by her tone that it was her final word, at least for the moment. "Mom, Dad, I can't talk anymore right now. Let me know when you're ready to listen."

And she hung up. Then she cupped her hands and held her face there, as if her head was just so heavy. I crept away so she wouldn't know I'd been there. I found J.R. dozing in a spot of sun by the back door. I lay down beside him, and he thumped his tail. I felt bad that my mom was fighting with Grandma and Grandpa, but I was happy she'd stuck up for me. J.R. sighed like he'd had a really hard day, even though all he'd done was sleep. I wondered if he was bored. I stroked the velvety spot on his nose.

"Ya wanna go out, boy?" I asked him, and J.R.'s whole body came alive, starting with his tail. I went to get his leash. Keeping J.R. happy was so simple.

The next day I discovered that the Ravens' uniforms were black and red. The coach tossed them to us one by one. Two of the kids missed the catch. I tried not to worry that they bobbled a slow-moving T-shirt coming at them. Coach Vijay Goel had a brown, smiling face and a bucketful of baseballs. He said we could call him Coach Vij.

We all stood around in a circle to get the team details. The first practice is always boring stuff like schedules and uniforms and which parents are going to do scorekeeping and field prep and on and on. The practice was at the same park where I'd met Hank, so just a few blocks from my new house. The league was co-ed, but there were no girls on the Ravens that I could see. Maybe there were some on the other Redburn team, which was called the Rockets. The other teams in the league were from the surrounding suburbs and made up of any other kids who wanted to play ball on the off-season. If you thought there *was* an off-season, unlike Nana.

"What's the first rule of Ravens baseball?" asked Coach Vij, surveying the group. I noticed Hank fiddling with his Mariners cap.

"Don't talk about Ravens baseball!" shouted one kid. He was small and pale, and I didn't hold out high hopes for him. It wasn't his build or his *Fight Club* joke that I found discouraging. It was the way he'd been picking at the grass and stretching his gum out of his mouth. I pegged him as a kid whose parents made him play. That's the worst. Their parents don't want them glued to *Minecraft* all summer, so some baseball team gets them. They sit down and rest in the outfield and spend the whole time in the dugout talking about what they're going to buy from the concession when the game is over. Not that I am against a killer hot dog and a freezie, but still.

"No, Oscar, the first rule is that we have fun."

"Knew it!" shouted Hank, suddenly awakening from his zombie trance. The names went by so fast that I didn't catch them all, except for Oscar, Arjun (the coach's kid—everyone called him A.J.) and Hank, of course. There was a big guy named Gus. I hoped he could hit. Every team needs power hitters. I was good at making contact, but I couldn't always belt it. My super power was that I had fast wrists. Every coach had told me so.

"So," Coach Vij was saying, "my parents loved baseball, and now both my kids love baseball.

My wife plays, my little daughter plays, and A.J. here, of course. The Goel family is usually on a ball diamond somewhere. I even proposed to my wife at Dodger Stadium. We got on the kiss cam."

"Dad!" said A.J., looking like he'd just found a nest of baby rats in his lunch bag. Like the team didn't need to hear about that romantic stuff.

"Sorry! Okay, team, time to get moving! A.J., you hand out the hats. Let's start things off with a jog to warm up, and then we'll review the basics. Meat-and-potatoes baseball—catching, throwing and batting."

"Coach Vij," said Oscar, shooting his arm up. "I'm a vegetarian."

Why did that not surprise me? He looked like someone who could use a real hot dog.

"That's okay, Oscar," said Coach Vij, sighing. "It's just an expression."

I put my Blue Jays cap in my baseball bag and pulled on my new Redburn Ravens one. It fit just right. I jumped into all the practice drills. I jogged, I hit, I threw, and then I sprinted bases. I felt like me in my boy clothes. I felt like me in my boy walk, slouchy and low to the ground. I forgot all my worries about school, and where I would go to the bathroom, and whether anyone would ever find out my secret. When it was my turn to hit pitches from Coach Vij, I stood at home plate and found my spot in the box. I was ready. *Pop, crack, pop.*

"Nice job, Caspar. You've got fast wrists."

I just smiled and helped collect the stray balls. My dad told me it's good to be humble because there is no *I* in team. I knew the other boys would be sizing me up.

After practice I walked home with Hank. He talked nonstop about the coach, our team and our chances for the season.

"Dude," he said. "With Gus's swing and your arm, we are *sooo* going to beat the Rockets this season."

"It's just summer ball." I shrugged, trying to keep it cool. I liked to win, but more than that I wanted to be part of a team that worked together. It sucked to feel like you were the only one trying.

"The Rockets hate the Ravens. There's always this thing about which team is best in Redburn. The other teams don't matter that much."

"I get it," I said. Rivalry in the neighborhood. It made sense.

"Hoo-hoo," Hank said. "We are going to be kings of the diamond." He held up a fist for me to bump.

I bumped back. I was glad he was excited. But, as Nana always reminded me, you should never count your Ws before the end of the ninth.

That night I finally got a message from Matt, via my dad's email. My dad let me sit at his computer in the office, which was still filled with boxes. He left me alone to read it.

> *Dear Caz,*
> *How is Washington? Do you like your new house?*
> *I played in a Fun Tournament. It wasn't that fun. It was a blowout and not for my side.*
> *How is your swing? I got a new Xbox game called* Field Day *where robots attack during a baseball game. Do you root for the Mariners now?*
> *We all miss you.*
> *Write back,*
> *Matt*

I read it twice, and then read the third-to-last line three times. *We all miss you.* I wondered who really missed me. Matt did. We'd been best friends since first grade. Whenever we'd gone away, his family had looked after J.R. for us. He'd stood up for me when no one else did. Well, most of the time.

"Dad," I called, "can we Skype with Matt?" On our last night in Toronto, we'd had a barbecue with Matt's family, and he and I had both cried. Then our moms had hugged each other and cried. We'd promised we would write and Skype.

My dad appeared at the door, balancing a bowl of ice cream on one palm.

"I'm sorry, Caz. It's way too late in Toronto. Matt will be asleep. Another time, okay?"

"Okay."

He disappeared again, the sound of a spoon clattering. I started to write an email back, to assure Matt my swing was fine and that I still rooted for the Jays. Then I remembered walking into Matt's kitchen the night of the barbecue to get us some sodas. The screen door was propped open. Matt's mom and my mom were leaning against the counter, talking, wineglasses in hand.

"It's going to be so hard, Elaine," my mom had said. It came out more like a sob.

Matt's mom had hugged my mom, and the white wine sloshed in their glasses.

"Maybe," said Matt's mom. "But you are all more than up for it, especially that great kid of yours."

I'd crept back out to Matt's backyard, my bare feet tickled by the dry summer grass.

"Where are the sodas?" he asked.

I shrugged, not able to say.

"I'm sorry for what happened," he blurted.

I'd stared at him for a second. He looked scared, like I was going to yell at him.

"Me too," I said.

We'd ended up bouncing on Matt's trampoline, chucking Wiffle balls at each other and laughing like five-year-olds. When it got dark and the parents were still talking, Matt and I had lain on the trampoline, looking up at the sky. I'd wondered if the stars would look different in Washington and if I would meet another friend with a trampoline. Then I had felt bad for thinking that, as if I were forgetting about Matt already.

Second Inning

Game day. I could tell right away that the Redburn Rockets were a tight team. The first thing I saw when I got to the park was player number 9 cranking a ball their coach had pitched. The coach had one of those big, thick beards that are in style—or, at least, that lots of guys wear. When number 9 turned around, he caught me watching and saluted.

"Watch and learn," he said to me through the wire fence.

It was that kid from the tryout, the one who had switched the For Sale sign on the cars. Kyle something. I held his stare for a moment so he would know I wasn't afraid of him. Then I went and found the Ravens dugout. The ground was sprinkled with sunflower shells from the last game. Baseball players are crazy for sunflower seeds. My mom hates finding the shells in the laundry.

I was the fourth to arrive. A.J., Coach Vij and Oscar were already there, tossing the ball.

"Caspar! Excellent. You can partner up with Oscar and do some grounders. But first, can you take the batting order over to the scoring booth for me?" The batting order was usually scratched on a slip of paper in pencil, old school, in case some kid didn't show up at the last minute.

"Yes, Coach." I ran to climb the stairs to the little booth behind home plate. Hustle is important. I took a peek at the paper and saw my name in the ninth position. I'd get fewer at-bats. But that was okay. I was the new kid. I'd have to prove myself to the coach and everyone else who had played the previous year. A man sat at a table by the window overlooking home plate. He was bent over a laptop, frowning.

"Coach wanted me to give you the batting order," I said, holding out the paper.

"Thanks. I'm Kent Budworth, scorekeeping for the Rockets. I'm just trying to get this app started up. And you are…?"

He smiled at me. He was wearing those glasses that change in shade or light.

"Caspar Cadman. I play for the Ravens. We just moved here."

"Well, welcome to Redburn. And good luck today."

"Thank you, Mr. Budworth," I said, then headed back to our dugout.

Oscar had spotted a wasp zagging at him and was running around like it was a yellow ball of fire. He was wearing the short baseball pants, the ones Nana said looked like knickers. I tried not to stare as his legs eggbeatered away from that wasp.

"I'm all-*er*-gic!" he shouted.

Oscar had a lot going on. But he was super quick. He'd be a natural for stealing bases. It was good to have someone fast. Oscar was a little unusual, but his speed could definitely be an asset.

The rest of my team showed up pretty much all at once. We lined up for drills—kicking our heels to our behinds, then swinging our legs forward to touch our toes. I was learning names. Besides Hank, A.J., big Gus and Oscar, there was a guy named Patrick who was apparently a wicked pitcher. And Kahlil, Dwight and Jerome. Not bad, eh? I have a good memory for names and statistics. If you ever need an answer to a baseball trivia question, try "Joe DiMaggio." It's as good a guess as any.

We were the home team, so we were out on the field first. I was playing left field, which was fine by me. Best to stay in the background for a bit. Patrick was on the mound. If the Rockets were so tough, I assumed Coach Vij would be hoping for a strong start to set the tone. Patrick struck out the first batter after what my old coach would have called a "battle royale" at bat. The player, who was small but scrappy, kept fouling off. The sound was like a kernel popping.

The second batter, wearing a bright orange helmet, got thunked on the elbow as he turned, which earned him a hit by pitch. One on first. One out. The next batter hit a hopper toward third base, which Gus bumbled, allowing the runner to reach first. Double bummer. There were two batters on base and only one out. We needed to get some outs fast.

Up next was someone I recognized: Kyle Loudmouth. He was batting cleanup, the number four spot. Maybe Kyle was as good as his swagger suggested. Coach Vij gave the outfielders a wave to back up—heavy hitter. I could see Patrick was rattled. He stopped to take several deep breaths. Kyle, who looked more like thirteen than under eleven, stood away from the plate and took a practice swing. It was a good cut, like a hungry giant swiping the air with a spoon. Patrick threw hard. Swinging strike. I had a bad feeling about this Kyle guy.

Ball, ball, ball. C'mon, Patrick, I thought, don't let him on your island. Steel and oak, steel and oak.

Patrick threw a sinker. Kyle took a massive swing and fouled it out over the fence, the ball thumping the top of a gray minivan with a convincing crack, causing the van's alarm to go off.

"Son of a monkey!" an adult shouted, jumping from the bleachers and sprinting to the van. Now that was hustle.

Score that one as an error on the minivan owner.

We were at a full count, three balls and two strikes. Things were about to get interesting. Patrick wound up and launched a missile. Kyle, out of chances, swung, and when I heard the ball make contact I started moving. I had a feeling. I tracked the ball as I ran, my glove at the ready. The ball soared toward the top of the wire fence. Just as it was about to clear the fence, I sprung up into the air and stretched my glove like someone reaching for an apple at the top of the tree. I fell to the ground, hard, but kept my glove in the air, still squeezing the ball. I sprang to my feet and threw as I hard as I could, all the way to third. It wasn't my best throw, but Gus was tall enough to snag it.

"Tag him!" A.J. called from right field. Gus remembered what to do and chased the runner who had tagged up at second. The orange-helmet runner froze seeing Gus charging at him. Gus made the tag.

"*Yessss!*" I heard someone shout, probably Hank. "Double play!"

The inning was over. I had made my first play and my first double play. Judging by the look Kyle shot me as he went to the dugout, I had also made my first enemy.

Kyle made sure I knew what he thought of my messing up his home run. In the third inning he hit me on the shoulder with a pitch. In the fourth inning, when I was playing second base, he knocked me to the ground while he was running, even though I wasn't on the base path. The ump didn't call it, because why would Kyle have done it on purpose? Anyone who thinks baseball is non-contact should watch Kyle and the Rockets play. Hank had warned me how rough they were. It was a frustrating game. In the sixth inning an ump called a Rocket safe when he stole home, even though A.J., who was playing catcher, had clearly made the tag. The kicker was when I made a throw to Oscar at first base just as an airplane flew overhead. Oscar looked up to the sky, and the ball thumped past him.

"You catch like a girl!" I heard someone shout from the Rockets dugout.

"Hey!" their coach shouted. "There'll be none of that."

In the final count we lost to the Rockets 15 to 9. Not quite a blowout, but not good either. We had some strikeouts, a few groundouts and a couple of pop outs. We just couldn't get our bats together. So much for hitting the sticks. It was more like getting hit with sticks.

"You made some great plays out there, Ravens. You're starting to act like a team. Gus, Caz, your double play was awesome. I like the way you're talking to each other, calling the ball, backing each other up. We've got some work to do on our hitting, but hey, I'm here all summer."

I could cope with losing. I didn't like it, but it happened. I dreaded having to tell my parents though. My dad had been working, and I'd asked my mom to sit this one out—it would have amped my nerves. I didn't want to relive the whole thing.

"Great game today, Caz," said A.J. as we gathered up all the equipment. "That was some catch."

"Thanks. That was a monster double you had in the third."

I had missed talking baseball. Hank appeared, reading the joke on a Double Bubble wrapper. He handed a piece of gum to A.J. and one to me. We unwrapped and bit into the gum, which was like hard pink concrete. While we chewed, we had to endure one last cheer from the Rockets.

"*We're Rockets, we rule! We're taking you to school!*

"*We can't be beat, so take a seat. We'll show you who's the boss.*"

"That doesn't rhyme," noted A.J., producing a bubble the size of a grapefruit. He had big brown eyes and long dark eyelashes that Grandma Ames would have said were wasted on a boy.

"Last year they had a cheer about kicking teams in the butt, but Coach Cronck made them change it," added A.J.

"What'd they rhyme *butt* with?" asked Hank.

"Let's just get going," I said to him, shouldering my baseball bag. It was red and white, with my last name stitched on the side. It had been a special bag for the Red Devils. I'd "played up" because I'd only been nine and most of the others were ten.

"Cool bag, Cadman," said A.J. and ran off to join Coach Vij at their car.

The Rockets were finally done celebrating, and Kyle sauntered past. He was slurping from a green Gatorade water bottle that had *Budworth* written on it in black marker. Then I realized that Mr. Budworth, the guy in the score booth, must be his dad.

"Nice game, ladies," Kyle said to us as he went by, swinging his water bottle. For some boys, calling someone a girl is the worst thing they can come up with. Don't guys have a mom? I had nothing against girls. I just knew I was a boy.

"Ya wanna walk home together?" asked Hank.

"Sure," I said. And for once we didn't even talk about baseball. Hank had a lot to say about rock-climbing, something else he apparently excelled at, and he gave me the rundown on the teachers at Redburn Elementary, even though school was the last thing I wanted to think about.

When we got to my house, J.R. was peering out the living-room picture window, which meant he must be up on the couch. He'd get in trouble for that. He disappeared from view, probably to race to the door to greet me. He'd seemed a bit nervous since we left Toronto. It was the only home he'd ever known too.

"See ya, Caz," said Hank. "Hey, my parents say you can come sleep over sometime."

"Cool," I said, but my stomach flopped over. "I'll ask my mom."

We did a fist bump.

My mom asked me all kinds of questions about the game, no doubt trying to gauge if the kids were being nice to me. Yes, unless you counted Kyle— but I wasn't going to mention him. She worried.

When it was time for bed, I got into my favorite striped pajamas. J.R. sauntered in to flop down by my bed. I thought about how baseball was always a game of "what ifs." What if I hadn't swung at that junk pitch? What if I hadn't popped out to close that inning? What if the ump had called that ball a strike? *What if, what if, what if?* A lot of baseball couldn't be controlled.

What if I had just been born a boy? Would I still be me, Caspar? What if Hank somehow discovered the truth at a sleepover? J.R. let out a loud snore. He was pretty lucky to be able to fall asleep without any "what ifs." J.R. was a good example of how to be super chill. He always made me feel better, and he was always my friend, no matter how I hit or what I wore or even how I smelled. That was the best way for a friend to be.

Third Inning

Coach Vij gave us a pep talk. It was totally inspirational, like a YouTube clip or something. Best of all, I knew he meant it. For his day job, Coach Vij was a real estate agent. His signs were all over Redburn. But you could tell he lived and breathed baseball. And if he had to put up with odd ducks like Oscar or even Dwight (who had tried to sneak a Game Boy into the dugout), so be it. We'd already faced the toughest team in the division, the rival Rockets, so I think Coach figured we might come out with a W against the Belleford Bruins. I was a little punchy because my mom and dad were in the stands. Dad had joked that he was going to live-tweet it for Nana Cadman.

"Take a knee," said Coach Vij after we'd finished our warm-up.

Most of the team sat down, their ankles against their behinds.

"One knee!" said Coach Vij, looking exasperated. He waited while everyone adjusted.

"Ravens," he began, "are not strong or big, but they are wily creatures."

"I saw a nature special on them!" shouted Oscar, who seemed to have no sense of volume with his voice. "They can play xylophones!"

"Not now, Oscar," said Coach Vij, waving his hands for emphasis. I could totally imagine him selling houses. "Ravens use their skills. They don't need to be big, because they are highly intelligent."

I saw where this was going. We weren't a team of big guys, except for Gus. I was pretty tall, but no one would call me stocky.

"Ravens also thrive by working together. They adapt, and they even show empathy to each other."

"I'm here for you, Caz," cooed Jerome, who was kneeling at my side. Jerome was always horsing around. He did show signs of being a good player when he paid attention.

"I want you all to play like Ravens," said Coach Vij, ignoring Jerome. "You play smart, you use your skills, you work as a team, and you support each other."

I raised my hand. "Ravens are tricksters," I said, remembering a First Nations story we'd read in school.

"Exactly," said Coach Vij. "Let's keep them off-balance. Let's surprise them with how well we play as a team."

We leaned in for a cheer. "*Goooo*, Ravens!" We were the visitors today, so first to bat. Hank and Oscar were at the top of the order. While Oscar was putting on his helmet, I made a small suggestion.

"Hey, O, remember how we practiced bunts? You might want to try one today unless Coach gives you a sign. You're so fast, dude."

Oscar nodded, his face bleached of color. He got super nervous before he batted. I hadn't seen him make contact in a game yet.

Hank was leadoff and hit a dribbler between the mound and first base, the worst positioning imaginable. Unbelievably, the Bruins pitcher lost hold of the ball, giving Hank enough time to beat the throw to first. I heard my mom holler, "Great hustle, Hank!"

You wouldn't know it to look at her, because she's pretty small, but my mom can really yell. She could be an ump, no problem. Then I heard Jerome call out, "Way. To. Go. Hank." He liked to use a robot voice.

Whatever. Chatter was good. It was part of being a team.

Up next was Oscar. He swung at a junk ball, spun around and nearly fell over onto the catcher.

"Oscar!" shouted Coach Vij. "Back up in the box!"

Oscar nodded stiffly, as if agreeing to a seat in the electric chair. I got ready for my own turn, fastening my helmet (classic black with silver trim) and my batting glove (red and white).

Oscar stared hard at the pitcher, and I realized that he really did care about the game. That made me feel better. I just couldn't stand it when players didn't try. Then a pitch, a little *pop*, and Oscar had executed a pretty good bunt. He ran his pants off, those short legs flying to first. Safe. Hank got to second and then sprinted to steal third on an overthrow. He stood there beaming like a glow stick. I gave him a thumbs-up. Now we had runners on first and third—men at the corners, as Nana would say.

Jerome was up next, and I stepped out of the dugout to get on deck. I watched the pitcher, who was a tall gangly kid with long blond hair flowing down from his helmet, like that Mets pitcher. I couldn't believe we had two on base, and I think Coach Vij was surprised too. He had a dazed half smile on his face.

I took a practice swing. I watched the pitcher. I heard my mom utter a small "Go, Caz!" even though I wasn't even up yet. Embarrassville: Population, 1. Jerome had good hand/eye coordination, if not a burning interest in baseball. Maybe it was the video games—who knew?

"Jerry," I called. "Let's go! Hit Hank home."

"What?" asked Jerome, turning toward me. "No one calls me Jerry!"

"I just did!" I shouted.

That seemed to take the edge off, because Jerome settled in to battle the Viking-like pitcher to a full count. *Foul, foul, foul, foul,* and then *kish!*—a hard hit down the right foul line. It was good! The first baseman whipped it home, so Hank stayed on third. I was up to bat with the bases loaded.

"C'mon, Caz, grand slam!" called my dad.

Why did he have to do that? Now it would never happen. Did he understand nothing about baseball superstition? I admit it, with the bases loaded I was nervous. Tiny moths darted around in my stomach.

"C'mon, Bruins, let's beat these losers!" yelled some grown-up from the home bleachers, clearly tired of seeing us on the bases. He obviously hadn't read and signed the parent-conduct form from the baseball association. You had to promise to always be a good sport, encourage fair play and not force your kids to play baseball. Almost all the parents broke the rules at some point.

"Hey, not okay!" my mom yelled before my dad shushed her. As I said, my mom sometimes gets a little intense at games.

I took my time, not letting anyone rush me. Despite trying to be cool, I swung at a junk pitch. Stupid. The Viking had me chasing, just like he wanted. I'd never admitted it to anyone, but I was always a bit scared when the ball barreled at me. It hurts to get hit. I was afraid of striking out too, especially in front of my new team. I didn't want them to think I was a loser. I wanted them to—

Strike!

I'd missed another one. Two strikes.

"If you like it, give it a rip," shouted Coach Vij.

"Go, Caz!" yelled Hank from third.

The next pitch was wild and whizzed high by my head, whining in my ear like a mosquito. It nearly clocked me on the helmet, and I had to do the deep breathing Miss Linda had talked about because it reminded me of That Day. The one I kept trying to forget. *You're okay, Caz, you're okay. The pitcher didn't mean to hurt you, not this time.*

Not this time.

I froze, remembering that day in Toronto. The worst day ever. Another pitch came at me, and I didn't swing or move.

"Caz, next one is yours!" My dad.

"Enough farting around, Caz!" My mom. I wasn't sure if the word *farting* was allowed in the Redburn baseball club's code of conduct. She was usually quiet and shy with strangers, but she became a kind of baseball-mom leviathan at games. It was nice, because she seemed to forget her worries about me for six innings. It gave us all something else to think about.

I felt my head jump back into my body. Bases loaded. Two strikes, two balls.

"What is he waiting for, Christmas?" shouted someone from the bleachers.

The pitcher fluffed his blond hair off his shoulder and hurled a slow-moving hunk of junk my way. I faced a full count.

I noticed Oscar twitching around at second base, taking a lead, then jumping backward. What the— was he moonwalking? *Oscar, pay attention*, I wanted to shout, but a sweet heater was coming right at me. My brain told me it was good. I leaned on my back leg and took a big swing. *Crack!*

I ran on contact as I'd been taught, surprising Gus on first, who'd gotten sleepy. Coach Vij wind-milled his arm, shouting, "Go, go, go!" I'd hit the ball close to but not over the fence in center field—we'd have to hoof it. None of the other parents on the Ravens team knew my name yet, so all I heard was "Run, boy!" and "Attaboy!" Hank, Oscar and Jerome all scored. Coach was telling me to keep going, so I ran like I had red ants in my pants and slid into home just as the catcher caught the ball. He tagged me, but I'd already made it.

Safe.

The crowd roared on the Ravens side. There were a couple of stray boos from the Bruins fans who thought the catcher had made the tag. Hank, Oscar and even Jerome all came to slap me on the back.

"Way to go, man," said Gus, and I felt like I'd just been high-fived by Clayton Kershaw.

"And that's Caspar Cadman, number 3, with a grand slam," said the announcer.

"Caspar Cadman is a great baseball name!" I heard a fake high voice say.

I undid my helmet and scanned the bleachers. There was Kyle, wearing a green Rockets hoodie, sitting right by home plate with another dude in the same hoodie. Kyle had his hair parted and slicked down.

They were both holding cellophane bags and shoveling candy into their mouths. Kyle watched as I went back to the dugout. I could feel his eyes on me.

You don't have to apologize for being good, Cassie, my dad had told me once. *But always remember that you're part of a team.*

"That was a heaping slice of awesome," said Hank, his eyes shining.

"A-greed," said Jerome in his robot voice.

Oscar answered by doing the moonwalk along the dugout. He had it down. I just laughed because I was kind of proud of him, of us. We were holding our own against the Bruins, at least. But from what Hank had told me, the Ravens usually got clobbered by the Rockets, who had won the division championships two years in a row. I was hoping we could change that.

Despite our four early runs, the Ravens fell to the Bruins 11 to 8. Patrick pitched well, but our fielding fell apart in the fourth inning, and the other team feasted on our mistakes—a dropped fly ball, an overthrow. Someone homered with a simple line drive. It was ugly baseball. Then, in the final inning—our games lasted six—a bald eagle dropped into the middle of the field and started ripping apart a mouse with his talons. I just stood there with my mouth hanging open, like a real city boy. I had never seen anything like it. Everyone else glanced at the eagle but just kept playing, as if the bird was a regular at the ballpark. I fumbled a grounder, which cost us a run. Eventually the eagle finished its dinner and flew away, making a musical call like keys jangling.

Despite the loss, the mood in the dugout after the game was upbeat. All the guys were passing around bubble gum, and Jerome's mom brought home-made chocolate-chip cookies in a big plastic tub. We pounced on them, kind of like the eagle, as if they were the last cookies on earth.

"Great game, Ravens," said Coach Vij. "We need to up our D, not give them so many chances. But you played as a team, and you did what I asked. I want to give a special shout-out to Oscar, who got his first base hit with his first game bunt."

"First game bunt that worked," corrected Oscar. "And it wasn't the best bunt."

"If everyone had to be perfect all the time, nothing would ever get done," said Coach. I had never thought of it that way before.

"Yay, little O!" shouted Gus, slapping Oscar on the back. Oscar nearly dropped his cookie. We were all pretty happy, joshing around while we collected our gear. I could feel my mom and dad lurking outside the dugout, watching. That's why I liked the baseball diamond. It was my place. I never stood around wondering where to hold my hands or what to say. My mom waved, miming for me to remember my cap. Yes, I'd left a few ballcaps behind. *Thanks for embarrassing me again, Mom.*

"I'll meet you at the car," I called to her.

"Caz, that grand slam was the coolest," said A.J.

"Thanks, dude. You pitched a gem." It was true. He'd pitched a sweet inning. Patrick had pitched well too. We smiled at each other, and I felt for a second like I belonged.

As I lugged my gear to the car, I passed Kyle and his green-hoodie friend unlocking their bikes.

"Way to blow that grounder, Caz the Spaz," said Kyle, watching me walk by.

I felt my shoulders go stiff. I clamped my lips shut. The last thing I needed was a fight with this guy. *Steel and oak.*

Kyle's friend snorted a laugh. He was sucking on one of those candy ring pops, which made him look like an enormous hoodie-wearing baby. I tried not to laugh.

"Something funny, Spaz?"

I had all kinds of answers in my brain, like *Just thinking about your swing*, but instead I walked to the car, making sure to keep my head high.

"Were those boys friends of yours, honey?" my mom asked as I got into the car.

"No," I said and left it at that.

At dinner that night my parents were all hyped up about my grand slam, which my dad kept calling a "grand salami," and how nice the other kids on my team seemed. I almost forgot that we'd lost. I knew the Ravens weren't used to winning much, and maybe that was okay. My parents extended my bedtime a bit later than usual, after I had a big bowl of mint-chocolate-chip ice cream.

"Have a good sleep, Caspar," said my mom, coming in to give me a kiss. "You earned it. That was quite a game." She smoothed the back of my hair, where my braid used to be.

"Thanks, Mom." It was always safe to talk about baseball. We talked a lot about baseball in our house. My dad came in next, and after he left I heard them murmuring in the living room. I wondered what they said when I wasn't there.

Once I finally got into bed I couldn't fall asleep. My mind kept churning over things: what Kyle had said to me, the eagle eating the mouse in the outfield—which was kind of amazing and horrible at the same time—and everything that had happened back in Toronto before we moved.

Rain Delay

You may be wondering what happened after that haircut. I wore my ballcap to practice as usual, so it took a few minutes for my teammates on the Lightning to notice. In theory, girls were allowed on the team, but I was the only one that year. Most of the girls who had started in baseball had switched over to softball by my age. So if I bobbled a throw, I felt that everyone in the stands was rolling their eyes. If I hit a ground-rule double to the fence, everyone seemed super surprised, like, *What a novelty!* The fact that I was a girl was a big deal, even though everyone pretended it wasn't. When it was my turn to bat at practice, I pulled off my cap so I could fasten on my helmet.

"Cassie," said James, the first baseman for the Lightning. "You sure did a number on your hair. You totally look like a boy."

"I like it," said Matt quickly. "It's better for wearing a batting helmet."

Matt knew I felt like a boy. Actually, I'd *told* him I sometimes felt like a boy. I hadn't wanted to tell him the whole truth, that I *always* felt like a boy.

"I think she looks like a boy," said James, standing his ground as usual. I didn't know James that well, only that that he was stubborn and sometimes lost track of his strikes and balls when he was batting— but he would never admit this. He also played hockey, and sometimes I wondered if his heart was really in baseball like mine was.

"Can you guys call me Caz all the time instead of Cassie?" I asked, all in one big breath, afraid of what they'd say.

"Totally like a boy," said James, as if we hadn't heard him the first time. I wanted to look like a boy. I just didn't want everyone talking about it.

"Girls can play baseball, you know," said Eddie, who was usually the catcher.

Of course I knew that. Girls could play baseball. I just didn't *feel* like a girl. I realized it was going to be impossible to explain all this to them. They were never going to get it—get *me*.

"Just call me Caz, okay?" I said, and then it was my turn to bat.

That's when it started. While I was batting, someone started singing that "Dude (Looks Like a Lady)" song, which didn't even make any sense but caused me to miss my pitch. The day before, we'd been working together on our run to win the championships. Now they were making fun of me. How could that happen because of one haircut?

Pressure is what makes diamonds, Nana Cadman once told me. That and carbon dioxide. She said something special often comes from being in a situation where you have to tough it out—like my mom being in labor for eleven hours, and eventually out came me! Nana was no geologist, but she did usually have good advice. She said your best friends will be there with you through thick and thin. So I finished the practice, and the one after that, despite the whispers. We didn't need the distraction. The regular season playoffs were coming up.

Our coach planned an extra practice the day before our first game. It was hot, but it went well. No one said anything strange, and I thought maybe they were getting used to the new me. We finished the regular practice, the coaches packed up and went home, and a few of us stayed behind to play a game of 500. My parents often picked me up a few minutes late, because they knew I loved 500—playing just for fun as the summer night cooled down and the sky began to fall dark.

The way we played was simple. One person batted, and the others tried to catch their shots. You got different points for your catch—100 if you grabbed it clean, 50 for grounders and so on. Once someone reached 500, they switched places with the batter. James put on his batting helmet over his long brown hair—he was growing it all feathery. Obviously he was going to bat first. We played for a few minutes, just four of us, as James batted. The ballpark was rimmed with backyards, and I heard a mom calling a kid home. Someone else was playing a radio on a porch.

"Nice hit, James," I said as I caught it in my glove. No bounce. That was 100 points. James just scowled at me. I should have known something was wrong then.

I caught a couple of fly balls, and Eddie caught a few, and Matt got some grounders. I picked up two grounders. Then James hit a line drive, *thwick*, right between Eddie and me. I dove for it into the grass and snagged it in my glove.

"Five hundred!" I called, standing up to dust myself off. That meant James could play while I batted.

"You're really a show-off, Cassie," said Eddie. "That was my mine to catch. You didn't even call it."

"That's not my name," I said, confused. I looked over at Matt. He shook his head, but I didn't know what that meant—*no, don't say anything* or *no, that's not your name*?

"Yeah, and I think you have trouble with math since you cut your hair, because there's no way that's 500."

"She's cheating. She didn't used to cheat when she was a girl." There was so much wrong with that sentence that I couldn't think of what to say. I actually couldn't even speak. I felt as if a panicked horse were galloping on my chest, trapped there, trying to find its way out.

"Guys, we're supposed to be a team," said Matt, walking over from right field.

"Tell that to Cassie the show-off," said James, glaring at me. "Oh, sorry—*Caz*."

"What did I do?" I asked, staring down at my glove as if the answer might be there.

Something had changed. *I* had changed. And they didn't like it.

"Let's just go, Caz," said Matt, tapping his sports watch. "It's time anyway."

We walked home in silence, the sound of my baseball cleats ticking against the sidewalk. Each step reminded me of the new names I had been called—*show-off, cheater.*

Finally, just as we reached the junction where we went our separate ways home, Matt cleared his throat.

"They're just jealous, Caz, because you're a better player than them."

I nodded, trying not to cry. You'd never see Joey Votto cry. I just wanted to get out of there.

"How was practice?" called my dad from the living room when I finally got home.

"Great," I lied. I could not tell them what had really happened. I could not begin to explain.

"Want to watch the game with me, pal?" asked my dad.

"Nah," I said. "Too tired." I admit it—I went to my room and cried, burying my head under my pillow as if that could make my thoughts go away. J.R. bumped the door open and barged in to see me, as if he knew I was sad. I fell asleep in my base-ball clothes and had a dream that I was trapped in a steamer trunk—the heavy kind with buckles that you take on long journeys. I tried knocking on the lid from the inside, and even though I could hear footsteps around me, no one helped me.

Nana Cadman appeared at our front door the next morning, carrying a paper bag of bagels from the bakery. The bagels were still warm.

"Fuel for the superstar," said Nana, smiling and placing the bag on the kitchen table next to my untouched glass of orange juice.

"Please don't call me that, Nana," I said.

Her smile disappeared. She was wearing the baseball earrings she liked to put on for games.

"I'm sorry, Nana," I said. "Thank you for the bagels. I'm just feeling…" I wasn't sure what to say.

"Nervous about the game?" she finished.

"Something like that," I said, tracing my finger through the condensation on the orange-juice glass.

"Win or lose, what's the worst that could happen?" asked Nana.

I thought about it. *Everyone laughs at me. I let my team down.*

"Mascot fight?" I said, to make her laugh. We'd seen a YouTube video of two minor-league mascots, an otter and a black bear, duking it out, except they were both too fat in their costumes to land a punch. It ended up being really funny.

"Just try your best, Caz. That's all anyone can ask. Hold your head high. Cadmans never give up, you know. Remember what pressure makes?"

"Pressure makes diamonds," I recited, reaching for the bagels.

∽

When we got to the game, the first of the regular season playoffs, I asked the coach to write my name on the lineup as Caz Cadman, because I didn't want to hear "Cassie" over the loudspeaker. Everyone knew something was up. The announcer said my name but pronounced it in this funny tone like, "*Heeere*'s Caz," and a few people laughed. My mom and dad and Nana Cadman just sat there in the stands, looking confused.

"What kind of name is that?" I heard someone mutter. "Didn't number 3 used to be a girl?"

I knew then, standing at home plate, that most of the Lightning players weren't really my "through thick and thin" friends. They had tolerated a girl on their team when my arm helped them win, but now? I froze at the plate, just long enough.

Strike one.

I replay that strike sometimes, because that is when I knew. *Caz, you are on your own.* Then it happened. The second pitch was coming straight for me—not my bat, but my head. I spun fast and got struck on the top of my shoulder. It felt as if someone had dipped it in fire.

The pitcher was glaring at me. He was heavyset and at least a head taller than me, with chocolate freckles and an overbite. His name was McGillan, but everyone called him Big Mack. I knew he was friends with James. They played on the same hockey team.

Sorry, Big Mack mouthed, then smiled.

That smile showed one thing—the hit was intentional. Since I'd been hit, it was a dead ball. I took a base. No one made a stink about me getting a beanball. No one clapped when I walked to first base. The whole diamond was silent, like the sound of snow falling. Then, when the next Lightning got a base hit, I ran to second base wondering if anyone besides Matt still had my back.

Was it wrong to cut my hair and ask to be called Caz? I was so tired of feeling like nothing about me felt right—my hair, my name, my clothes. I had thought my team would understand. I'd known most of the Lightning since we were little. They must have all been put in the right bodies when they were born. Why was it so wrong that I wanted the same thing?

Matt was up to bat and managed to get to first on a line drive. I ran to third, beating the throw. Big Mack was getting rattled. Too many batters were getting hits off him. Eddie was up to bat now, and Mack lobbed a wild pitch. The catcher bumbled it and then went lumbering off in pursuit, super slow, like some Stone Age tortoise.

"Caz!" I heard Nana Cadman yell. "Run like ya mean it!"

I fell back into my body, and I hightailed it for home, kicking up the dust. I slid and made it, just before the catcher swooped in for the tag. I heard my mom and dad cheering and Nana loudest of all.

I stood and dusted myself off. My run had nudged us into the lead of the first playoff game. I had done something. I had helped my team. I let myself feel a flicker of pride.

"You're still just a girl," the catcher said to me, as if reading my mind.

And things just kept going downhill from there. We won the game, but my teammates acted weird around me, like they couldn't look at me. The day before my tenth-birthday party, my mom fielded a flurry of emails from parents canceling. We'd booked a party at the batting cage and invited the whole team—ten players—as well as two girls from class that I'd known since preschool. It ended up being just those two girls and Matt. Everyone else on the Lightning suddenly had something else to do.

"More chances for us to hit," said Matt, but even he couldn't pretend it didn't suck. The saddest thing was seeing the enormous ice-cream cake my mom had ordered, back when she anticipated a crowd. It was shaped like a baseball. My new name was written on it in red icing. We barely made a dent in it. I can still picture that big melting cake. I told myself not to cry, and I didn't, mainly because I knew how sad it would make my mom.

It turned out my dad had already been offered the new job with the airline in Washington, and my parents had been weighing the pros and cons. Just before the school year ended, I went to class and found my desk stuffed with boys' underwear. It was supposed to be funny, I guess. I stared and left it all there. I heard a roar of laughter. Everyone saw and no one said a thing—not Matt and not my teacher. I ran from the room without even asking permission. I didn't tell my parents about it until a full day later.

I was just sitting there, staring at my dinner.

"Caz," my mom said, standing up from her chair and reaching to clear my nearly untouched plate, "tell me what is going on with you."

I burst into tears, and I told her. The next day my parents drove me to school, both of them wearing ironed clothes and proper shoes. We drove in complete silence. I don't know what the principal said, or what my parents said, but when I got home that night I could tell they weren't happy. That made three of us. I went straight to my room, in case they wanted to talk. I heard my mom slamming drawers in the kitchen as she started dinner. She was so angry that I could hear her fuming even from my room. Apparently the principal had told them that perhaps I should try to "toughen up."

When they called me for dinner, I came and sat down at my place.

"Let's go. Let's just go," I said. My parents knew exactly what I meant.

And two weeks and one Blue Jays game later, we left.

Fourth Inning

"I have a question for you," Coach Vijay said. Coach Vij was usually the one with the answers, not the questions. That's what I liked about him. I had too many questions. Like, how much longer would J.R. live? And what if my body started to look like a girl's? There was medicine I could take to stop that from happening, Miss Linda had told me. Mom said she had found a new Miss Linda at a clinic in Seattle and would set up an appointment in a few weeks.

I took a gulp of air. Could Coach Vij tell I was different? I wanted to be *good* different. Was I ready to explain? I could only say it the way I knew how—I was a boy. I knew that deep down in my body—the same way I knew when a clothesline throw would make it to first base. I just *knew*.

"Hey, Caspar, focus," he said, making the eye-to-eye point with his index finger. "Okay, here's the question. Or suggestion. I think you should pitch. Patrick and A.J. are both solid, but we could do with another arm."

"What?" I asked, surprised. "I mean, pardon, Coach?" My dad and mom had taught me to always be polite to the coach or that was it, I'd be outta there. They basically told me they'd keep driving me to games and practices, but I had to be a good sport and respect the game.

"I think you can do it. You've got the arm strength. You've got the accuracy. You're tall, which helps. You just need to get on the mound and practice getting it over the plate and into the strike zone. Then we can work on some fancier stuff."

"Really?" I asked, and realized I was smiling. I liked pitching, but it would mean a lot of eyes on me. Coach Vij thought I could do it.

"Really. Practice with your dad or mom, okay?" he said, in an Earth-to-Caspar voice.

I had a secret for Coach Vijay. I actually did know how to pitch. Heaters, curve balls, sinkers and even the weirdo slow Eephus, a junk pitch that confused batters. I hadn't ever pitched in a game though. Had that been because I was the only girl? I would never know. It would be a lot of pressure. But pressure is what makes diamonds, right?

The Ravens had improved to three wins, three losses. The summer playoffs were within striking distance. And here was the thing—we were getting better and better. Gus could always hit, but now he was making fielding plays. Oscar was getting on base with a combination of making contact and a fast dash to first. We didn't have big sinkholes in our lineups anymore. There were no players who always struck out and killed rallies. There was reason for hope. Coach Vij sensed it.

"Ravens, I'm thinking of taking our training up a notch. I'd like to add an extra practice on Monday afternoons, as well as our Wednesday and Sunday sessions. Would you like to do that?"

"Yes, Coach!" shouted Oscar.

"Thanks, Oscar," said Coach with a smile. "Actually, I was looking for a show of hands."

I put both my arms up. The only thing better than baseball was more baseball.

Coach Vij pretended to count the hands, but it was unanimous.

"Well then. I'll see you all at my Super Sunday practice. I'll have a surprise for you too."

Hank looked at me, eyes wide. Sometimes he was just like a little kid. He didn't worry as much as I did.

"Are you sure you're ready for this?" asked my mom. She'd left her job doing marketing stuff for a Toronto golf course when we moved, so now she could worry about me full time. I kinda hoped she'd find another job in Redburn eventually. For now, she said, she was going to chill with me for the summer. Her words.

"If I say no, it will hurt Hank's feelings," I said. I had already packed my new favorite pajamas— striped bottoms and a top with a baseball glove and ball stenciled on it.

My mom and dad had met Hank's parents, and they had been approved as nice people. I think Hank had been planning the sleepover since the first day he met me at the park. There had been no more talk of Grandpa and Grandma Ames visiting. It made me sad. I wanted to see them, but it seemed to me they wanted to forget about us.

"Okay, Caspar. That's very thoughtful of you," said my mom.

"I want to go," I added. I missed having sleepovers. The emails from Matt had tapered off a little. He was busy with the team, with camping, with all the things we used to do together.

I had my bag ready to go, even though it was only lunchtime. I would drive with Hank's family to their house after our Ravens practice for a swim in their pool, pizza, videos, and then to sleep in a tent in the backyard. It sounded awesome.

"Caspar?" my mom said, trying to sit down on my bed. She stood up again and tossed three comics, a roll of Mentos and a pack of baseball cards to the floor. Hey, I never said I was neat.

"Yes?" I picked up the pack of cards and tossed it in my bag. I wanted to show them to Hank.

"Are you going to tell Hank?" Her voice wobbled just a touch.

I thought for a minute.

"Not yet," I said. I knew my parents planned to tell the principal at my new school. Maybe I would tell Hank someday. But it didn't seem like the time.

"Oh no!" I said, slapping myself on the head, knocking off my Ravens cap. "Hank said to bring swim trunks."

My mom paused. She was probably thinking the same thing I was. We'd donated my last suit, a navy-blue one-piece, to the Salvation Army before we left Toronto.

"Well, we've got two hours before your practice. Let's go to Hardy's and buy you some trunks. We can get you another pair of baseball pants too. Look good for the playoffs."

My mom was smiling, but I could see a tear in the corner of her eye. I tried to remind myself that this was new for my mom. For a long time she'd thought she had a daughter, despite all the hints I had given her. In third grade I'd asked to race with the boys at a cross-country meet and everyone had let me, no questions asked.

My mom and I got in the car to go to Hardy's Sports World. J.R. was crushed that we left him at home, but it was too hot for him to wait in the car. In the air-conditioned store, I chose my first pair of swim trunks. They were surfer style, with a drawstring, and bright orange with a decal of a palm tree on the side. I found some baseball pants too. Then I spotted an awesome blue skateboard and managed to talk my mom into an upgrade. "Okay, why not?" she said, like some alien with an enormous bank account had entered her body.

"Does your son want to enter a draw for Mariners tickets?" the clerk asked as he rang up the goods.

Your son! He'd called me her son. It was like hearing the *pock* of a home run being hit.

"Pardon?" asked my mom, fumbling for her credit card. "Oh, Caspar, what do you think?"

"Sure," I said. It wasn't disloyal to the Jays to watch a Mariners game, especially if it was free. That was letting fate decide. My mom paid and then filled in the little slip. The clerk stuffed it in the contest ballot box. You could win tickets for yourself and ten friends. Did I have ten friends?

"You play for the Ravens?" asked the clerk, nodding at my cap. He looked to be about seventeen or eighteen.

"Yes," I said. I was learning it was sometimes better not to say too much when you were new.

"I used to play for the Rockets. You'd best practice up," he said, winking. He seemed pretty full of himself. Full of the glory of being a Rocket, I guess.

"Heading there right now," I answered, keeping my tone friendly. Baseball teams were like family tribes or something. You wanna know something about someone, you look at the hat.

My mom and I were pretty quiet on the drive to practice. She still sometimes got lost in Redburn and had to concentrate. I knew from experience that sometimes having everything be unfamiliar and new sort of hurt, like having a sunburn. I could only imagine what the first day of school would be like. My mom and I had gone to the school grounds a few times, walking J.R. She'd tried to get me to talk about school, what I expected and what I was afraid of, but each time I changed the subject. I don't like to talk much. I like doing. It was good hanging out with Hank. He did the talking—for everybody.

"Excited for the sleepover?" my mom asked as she made a left turn.

I nodded.

"A little nervous too?" she asked.

I nodded again. My mom knew me well.

We arrived at the park where our practice was scheduled, a bigger park that had two ball diamonds, washrooms and a playground with a spinning merry-go-round—the kind you hop on to ride. I used to love that. I saw that Rockets player, Kyle, jumping out of a minivan driven by the man I'd met in the score booth my first game. Mr. Budworth waved at me, a friendly salute, and Kyle pretended to wave too but mouthed, *You suck.* Either Kyle hated me or the rivalry between the

Rockets and the Ravens was on par with the Rebels and the Empire.

"This is such a friendly town," chirped my mom, pleased with all the greetings. "Have fun tonight, honey. Make sure you hydrate at practice, okay? It's hot."

We'd been having what counted as a heat wave in the Pacific Northwest. My mom knows I have a tendency to get wrapped up in playing and forget to drink water.

"I will, Mom."

As I shouldered my baseball bag and my backpack stuffed with sleepover gear, I suddenly worried that maybe Kyle had been transferred to the Ravens. He was a skilled player, but he had a hate-on for me, and I had begun to think of the Ravens as my friends. I didn't want Kyle to ruin that. Kyle was not a champion of the little guy, that's for sure.

Then I noticed that the Rockets were practicing in the smaller diamond over by the far fence. It was known as the Field of Dreams. (Every town has a ball diamond called Field of Dreams, I figure.) Great. They'd see our strategy and learn things about us they could use against us later. Like the fact that Oscar almost always has a new YouTube dance move to show us during our warm-up.

It seemed Kyle wasn't going to let me go peacefully to my practice.

"So, Cas*par*," he said, exaggerating the last syllable. "Do you have a dad?"

What did that mean? Kyle was clearly a foe, not a friend, but I was having trouble reading him. He seemed to have no goal except to bug me and throw me off my game.

"Yeah," I said, walking faster to my diamond. Jerome was there and also Kahlil, the lanky guy who always wore a chunky baseball necklace.

"I'll bet he's a florist or something. Or, like, a decorator with those rug samples," Kyle said, waving his hands around.

Sometimes guys like Kyle were only mean when they were with their meathead friends, but Kyle was doing just fine on his own. I knew he was trying to insult my dad. That was going too far. What was wrong with flowers anyway?

"Or maybe he's a jazz dancer. Is he a jazz dancer, Caz?" Kyle put his face right by mine. I'd reached my diamond.

"My dad's a pilot. He flies planes," I snapped, fed up, and I turned to hang my baseball bag on the fence. I put my backpack next to it. Just seeing my all-star team bag made me feel better. *Cadman*, it read in black stitching. *The Red Devils*.

You can do it, Cadman. Way to be, Cadman. How the crowd had cheered when I played for that all-star team. They liked me so much when I was helping them win.

Jerome and Kahlil were standing around shooting the breeze, talking about some Play Palace in a neighboring town where you could zip-line, play mini golf and rock-climb.

"Hey, Jerome, how's it going?" I asked him, trying to give Kyle the heave-ho.

"Caz, can you keep calling me Jerry? I kind of liked it."

"Sure thing, Jerry. Hey, Kahlil, Jerry, let's field some grounders while we're waiting for Coach. I can toss you some."

Kyle slunk off to the far diamond, scowling.

"Hey," I said to Jerome. "What is with that guy?"

"Kyle's just a mean dude." Jerome shrugged. "His dad owns a chain of hardware stores and donates money to our school for sports, so Kyle gets away with a lot. Mr. Budworth is okay though."

I nodded, feeling a twist in my stomach. I hated the thought of school. It was like this jagged black mountain looming in the distance but getting closer.

Coach Vij and A.J. and everyone else arrived in a big, noisy bunch. Coach seemed intent on ramping up the practices, as if he, too, realized we might have a chance at breaking the Rockets' winning streak, which sounded as if it went back to the pioneer days. "Talk to each other," he called to us. "Act like a team!" Halfway through the practice, all the water I'd been drinking caught up with me, and I hustled off to the bathrooms. I started to push open the door as Kyle came striding out.

"I wouldn't go in there if I were you," he said and ran off as if I'd held a barbecue lighter to his pants.

I looked at the bathroom sign with the skirt, and I looked at the one with the pants. I hadn't worn a skirt since I was six and Grandma Ames insisted I wear one to dinner at some boring steakhouse. I considered the possibilities for the boys' bathroom: dead rat, foul smell, bionic spider. The most likely scenario seemed to be that Kyle was jerking my chain.

I went in. I held my breath for a second and then exhaled. It was fine. I scanned the area—typical stalls and urinals. No spiders or rodents. I went into a stall and was back in time to join the game of scrub before it started.

"Hey, I want Caz on my team," I heard as I ran back, and I felt a little surge of something. I was happy.

∽

The door to Hank's house flew open before we even rang the doorbell. I held my sleeping bag in front of me, still rolled up. Hank and I grinned at each other. Then he realized being so eager was uncool, so he made his face more deadpan, and we fist bumped.

"Bye, Mom," I said, giving her a quick squeeze and scampering after Hank, my backpack with my pajamas and my swim trunks (my swim trunks!) bumping against my leg. Hank and I went to his room so I could inspect Mandy, his new tiger salamander. Mandy was black with yellow stripes and had beady licorice-black eyes. I heard Mr. and Mrs. Ottenburg talking to my mom—*Welcome to Redburn. Is Caspar allergic to anything?* All that grown-up stuff.

Hank leaned forward to pull Mandy from the tank. While Hank held the creature I ran one finger down its back, which was cool and damp.

"Is it a girl or a boy?" I asked, admiring the salamander's markings and webbed feet.

"I don't know. We got it off the Internet from someone who was moving to England. It was already called Mandy."

"Hi, Mandy," I said. Mandy froze, like a salamander mannequin. What was Mandy thinking?

"Mandy eats roaches and flies," said Hank, putting Mandy back in the tank. "Hey, wanna go swimming now?"

"Sure," I said, grabbing my bag. I headed for the bathroom before Hank could say anything. Hank's bathroom had one of those fuzzy mats, moss green, and I stood on it, staring at my toes as I changed. They didn't look like girl toes or boy toes. They were just toes.

I wore my swim trunks and a thin practice jersey from my old team. I didn't feel like baring my chest, not yet. I hitched the swim trunks up, then pulled them down slightly, so they rested on my hips. I liked them.

"Caz, let's *gee-oh* go!" shouted Hank. "I'm boiling!"

A minute later he was charging out to the backyard to do a cannonball into the pool. A second later I followed, flying feet first into the cold, rippling water.

∼

Dear Matt,

Got your message. Glad you are trying out for the Red Devils. You can do it! I know you can. Yes, Kevin is for sure full of himself, but he hits the homers. What can you do?

I went to a sleepover at my new friend Hank's last night. It was pretty cool. We played video games until his mom finally told us to knock it off, and we had blueberry pancakes in the morning. The Ravens are doing okay.

In other news, I got a new skateboard, kinda like yours. Wish we could go to the skate park together.

Your friend,
Caz

∼

Dear Grandma and Grandpa Ames,

Thank you for the baseball card of Robbie Alomar. Did you know he was a switch-hitter? He could bat left AND right.

Thank you also for the children's Bible. It has nice cartoons.

Love,
Caz

I felt weird signing my name *Caz* to my grandparents because they had never used my baseball name. They called me Cassandra or Cassie. I wanted to write Caspar, but I knew they wouldn't like it. I thought about signing it *C. Cadman*, but that would have sounded like I was running for prime minister or president or something, so I went with Caz. I couldn't go back to being Cassie, not even for them. That would be like walking backward to first base when you were already gunning your wheels to third.

Fifth Inning

I woke up Monday morning and realized I was smiling. This weekend I'd had my first sleepover as a boy, and today there would be baseball—the special practice. J.R. seemed to sense my good mood and trotted over to my bed for a pat. My mom had a few items on the agenda for the morning—dog walking, porch sweeping and weed pulling. Practice couldn't come soon enough. When it was time, I grabbed my baseball bag and flew out of the house, nearly shutting the door on J.R's tail.

When we got to the park I saw Coach Vij's car in the lot, but when the door opened Mrs. Goel stepped out, not him. She wore trackpants, a white workout top and a baseball cap. She was hefting equipment out of the car onto the gravel—the bucket of balls, helmets, extra bats. I waved goodbye to my dad and went to help.

"Hi, Mrs. Goel, can I help carry this stuff?" I asked. She turned, holding the bucket by the handle. Oh man, she was wearing a Marlins cap. I had never met anyone who loved the Marlins.

"Sure, Caspar, thanks," she said, handing me a cooler of water to carry to the dugout. The heat wave had continued. Everyone kept saying not to get used to it.

As we walked to the dugout, she asked me a bunch of questions, like how did I like Redburn, and what position did I like to play?

"Is Coach Vij coming?" I asked.

"Not today. He asked me to fill in for him today."

"You're the secret weapon?" I asked, grinning.

"Maybe," she said. "I've picked up some tricks."

Once the other players arrived, Mrs. Goel stood in front of the group. She tightened her ponytail and cleared her throat.

"Hey, team. Coach Vij asked me to run the practice today. You know that I'm A.J.'s mom, but today you can call me Coach Mira. We're going to warm up with a run, but first I have a question for you."

She paused for a moment. "Do you want to be winners or whiners?"

Silence. A jet was flying overhead, making a white streak across the sky. We all knew there was only one answer—but none of us could say it.

"What I mean to say is that you boys have gotten good this year, very good. You've worked hard. But do you think you're good enough to beat the Rockets after all these years?"

Silence again. True, the Cubs had finally won a World Series after decades of being shut out, finally justifying my dad's years of hard-core fandom. But did I think we were good enough? *Not yet.*

"There's still time," said Coach Mira. "But you're all going to have to focus. No sunflower seeds, no gum, no dorking around with Gatorade bottles."

Jerome whimpered a bit at that point. Those were his favorite dugout pastimes.

"I've got some special strategies to share with you. You should know that I don't share them with everybody."

Even Oscar seemed to pay attention to that.

"Okay, now let's do a warm-up. Three times around the field."

"Who roots for the Marlins?" muttered Hank as we fell into a line.

"Someone's got to," I whispered.

After the jog we practiced double plays and grounders, and Coach Mira helped some of the boys one-on-one in the batting cage. I wondered if Coach Vij was busy or if he'd put Coach Mira in to shake us up. Because she had. The practice was going awesome. Sometimes I felt I could play ball forever. Sometimes I believed I was born to play baseball.

"Okay, boys, well done," said Coach Mira.

What? I thought there were at least twenty minutes left in the practice. I figured we were calling it quits early. I turned to get my glove and help put away the equipment.

"Caspar, where do you think you're going?" she asked. The team all turned to me.

"Okay, Ravens, now I'm going to teach you the Stingray, my top-secret play. But first you must solemnly swear to never tell anyone about the Stingray. Now repeat after me. I promise…"

"*I promise*," we chanted.

But she wasn't done.

"To never tell…"

"*To never tell…*"

"Anyone, especially the Rockets, about the Stingray."

We all agreed, looking at each other with giant grins and shouting the *especially the Rockets* part as loud as we could.

The Stingray was epic. I would tell you about it. But I promised Coach Mira. Okay, I'll just give you the highlights. It involves faking a throw to second—but then you chuck it to the shortstop instead to get an out at home or at third. It is Strategy with a capital *S*. It is genius. I would wish Mira Goel was my mom if my own mom wasn't so awesome.

My dad came to pick me up in the car and seemed pretty amused by my enthusiasm for the secret play we'd learned and the practice in general.

"We're going places," I told him, a phrase I'd heard Nana use.

"How about going for ice cream with me?" he asked.

"So close to dinner?" I asked. I couldn't believe my luck. It was highly unlikely that my mom had approved this plan, so I didn't ask any more questions. I walked to the car, feeling almost giddy at the unexpected treat.

We ended up driving to a Dairy Queen about fifteen minutes away. I got a small soft serve—I didn't want to risk The Wrath of Mom.

On the way home we took a detour because my dad had to pick up a part for our lawn mower at a specialty hardware store.

"I'll just be a minute. Or you can come in with me," he said when he parked. Typical parent, letting you choose from two boring options.

"Hey, what's that, Dad?" I asked, pointing to a big field with netting. Then I realized it was a massive commercial batting cage, like the one in Toronto where I'd had my party. I noticed the sign—*Big Ned's Batting Cages.* If you were small, nothing was named after you, it seemed.

"Oh, yeah. I meant to tell you about that. We should go sometime. Looks busy though."

I looked closer and realized it was teeming with Rockets. I thought I saw a flash of Kyle's neon-orange baseball cleats off in the distance. It was almost certainly him.

By the time my dad came back with the part, the sugar high from the ice cream had worn off. The Rockets were swinging. And they weren't missing.

We would have to try harder. And I would have to pitch better.

I wasn't getting my windup the way I wanted. If it were a smell, it would be *eau de* summer dumpster. Seriously, it was bad. My dad wasn't making it any easier.

"Caz," he said, squatting down on our driveway and holding up a catcher's mitt. "Plant your back leg."

"I am," I said, whining like a little kid. I didn't remember my pitching ever being this bad. Maybe I just wasn't a good ballplayer at all, and the past had all been a fluke. Maybe—

"Caz," said my dad. "I am old, and I can only squat down for so long, so fire one in the glove. If you do, I'll give you a beer."

That, I knew, was not true. But I threw the ball anyway. It made a *thock* sound as it went into the glove. Ball high, an ump would have called.

"Not bad," my dad pronounced. "But hardly worth a beer." He pulled down his Cubs cap. No one could accuse him of joining a bandwagon when the Cubs got good. That cap was old and beat-up. He lobbed the ball back to me. I tried again.

"You know, Caz," he said, catching my throw, "girls can play baseball and be the best. Think of Mo'ne Davis."

Why was he bringing that up now? I knew all about Mo'ne Davis. My dad and I had watched tapes of her playing. She was amazing. Seeing her pitch a shutout at the Little League World Series was mind-blowing. I wished I could pitch like her.

"Mo'ne Davis is the best," I agreed. But then I looked at my dad's face. Something else was going on.

"Dad," I said. "Girls can rock baseball, but I'm not a girl."

People who grow up feeling right in their own body have a hard time understanding how it could feel wrong.

"Sorry, Caz. Sometimes I forget. You were my little girl for a long time." He looked down at the ground for a second. I felt like I was disappointing him, just like I was going to disappoint Coach Vij with these terrible pitches.

My dad threw the ball back to me, and I wound up and fired it back at him.

"Dad!" I shouted. "It's like I'm throwing flounders! I'm terrible!" I threw my glove down on the driveway, narrowly missing an anthill.

My dad laughed, which made me madder. "Flounders?"

"Like slow-moving fish," I said, and then I laughed too. It was kind of funny. Jake Arrieta had never thrown a flounder.

"Give me three more and then we'll take a break," he said.

The last one was pretty good—which was what my dad had been counting on. He's pretty smart. Hey, he knew the Cubbies would win eventually.

"I'll go get those beers," he said and went into the kitchen. He came back with two root beers in tiny bottles with foil caps, like champagne.

"This should be really good," he said. "I got it from that health-food store. When you win the championships, I'll dump some all over you, just like they do in the majors."

Redburn was pretty big on juice bars and no plastic bags and plenty of bike lanes and all that. When I'd heard we were moving to the States, I had wondered if I would meet people who owned guns, since there were so many on TV, but I hadn't seen one yet.

We sat down on the steps of the wooden deck. We'd left our old lawn furniture behind in Toronto. But I liked sitting on the steps. J.R got up from the shady spot he'd found under an azalea bush and we both patted him before he sauntered back.

"You miss Toronto?" my dad asked, taking a swig.

"Some things," I said. "The Jays are kind of stinko right now."

"They'll pull it together. They're too good not to," said my dad.

"Yeah, you're right," I agreed. My dad and I agreed on most things. We didn't fight much, except sometimes about the state of my room. It was an ongoing topic.

"Do you like your new job?" I asked. The root beer was sweet and cold. It was all-natural, made with cane sugar or something, but it was still super good.

"Most days," he said. "I miss some of my old co-workers. Sometimes I miss Toronto too, but it's cool living closer to the ocean. We could bike to the beach sometime with Hank, if you want."

"How about right now?" I asked.

He thought for a minute, holding the root-beer bottle in midair. "Give him a call."

"Awesome!" I said and ran to the phone. Hank, as usual, was all in, and my dad and I rounded up our bike helmets, towels and bathing suits. We left our baseball gloves behind. Maybe even the great Yaz went to the beach now and then on a sunny day.

Tuesday was a no-practice day, but a sunny afternoon without baseball was like naked fries with no ketchup. I called up Hank so we could practice together. Then Hank called up Oscar and Gus. We all met at the park and had our own mini practice. We practiced pop flies, did some grounders and even reviewed the Stingray. Then I offered to pitch so the others could get in some batting practice. We were just getting set up when I spotted some Rockets cutting across the field, heading our way. There were four of them. They were wearing their powder-blue uniforms, which reminded me of Grandma Ames's guest bathroom.

"We've got company," said Gus, squaring his shoulders. He sounded like a guy in a Western.

"I don't like company," said Hank, scowling.

"I always hafta clean my room when we have company," said Oscar.

"Let's just keep playing," I said. I was getting warmed up to pitch to the guys. I'd have to save my best stuff. I didn't want the Rockets to see it.

I was on the mound, ready to start pitching. Kyle headed straight for me. He stood a few inches away from me, right in my face. I hated that.

"You seem to be on our diamond," said Kyle.

I swallowed. "You seem to be standing on my mound."

"We've got some serious practice to do. So shove off." Kyle tapped me on the shoulder. I saw Gus bristle. Gus was a gentle giant, but it wasn't good to make him mad.

"We were here first," I said, keeping the shaking I felt from getting into my voice. "You can have it in half an hour when we're done batting."

"I don't see your name on this diamond," said Kyle. "We want it now."

I sighed, looking from Gus to Oscar to Hank. Gus looked fierce. Hank look worried. Oscar was sitting down by first base and trying to stab a straw into a juice box.

I took off my glove and set it down next to the mound. Then I put down the ball in my hand. I straightened my ballcap. Kyle clenched his fist. His whole body was quivering like a live electric wire. I stepped to one side and bent down in the dirt. I used my fingertip to spell out the letters of my name: *CASPAR*.

"There," I said. "Now you do. We'll be done in half an hour. In the meantime, there's space to practice over there." I pointed to the area at the far corner of the park. It was usually for younger kids—but it would do fine.

"Let's go, boys," Kyle said, gesturing to the corner practice area. "I don't wanna watch this anyway. This kid's gonna serve up more meatballs than The Old Spaghetti Factory."

I had to admit, that was a pretty good line. But back to work. Hank played catcher, and Gus was first up to bat. I had been afraid Kyle was going to slug me—and it took a few seconds for my hand to stop shaking. My adrenaline was still surging, and I threw a hard fastball. Gus swung and missed.

"Hoo. If that was a meatball, it was flaming!" yelled Gus, loud enough for the Rockets to hear.

"New team name!" shouted Hank. "The Flaming Meatballs!"

After a few pitches I got in the zone and almost forgot the Rockets were there. I looked at the watch Nana Cadman gave me for my birthday. It's shaped like a baseball and the second hand is a bat. I wanted to keep my word—half an hour, and then they could have the bigger field.

"Let's bring it in, Ravens," I called. In a softer voice, I said, "Look, we can come back tomorrow and practice again. I just don't want to start anything with them."

We packed up with five minutes to spare. The Rockets seemed a lot more interested in bugging us than actually practicing. By the time we left, two of them were just flipping their water bottles in the dirt. Kyle and another guy were throwing sunflower seeds at each other.

I wondered how we had ever let them beat us.

In baseball they say anything can happen. *Anything*. Trust me, it's true. If a major leaguer gets a ball stuck in his mitt, hey, he throws the whole glove to first base. And once, a ball beaned outfielder Jose Canseco on the top of his noggin—*boing!* He was okay, but it bounced over the wall, and the batter got a homer. Canseco was playing for the Texas Rangers. Just sayin.' A couple of years ago my dad and I watched a Blue Jays game that went *nineteen* innings! *Go to bed!* my mom hollered, but then she sat down and watched too. We just had to see how it ended. Now we had to see how the Ravens ended this year. We'd had our extra Monday practices as a team, and a small group of us had been meeting every day to play. Sometimes Hank looked at me and mouthed *Stingray* just because it was a secret we shared.

In our round-one afternoon playoff game against the Westlake Jets, Gus homered, and—get this—Jerome hit a line drive to far left field that earned him a double. Of course, Oscar also made a pretty tragic base-running error—causing a traffic pileup. I had played just okay. I singled, walked and struck out once, which didn't make me happy. I made a couple of good fielding stops. Still, I hadn't pitched yet in a game, though Coach had hinted I might. The Jets had an awesome girl on their team named Brooke—tall, orange cleats. She hit a ground-rule double, and she made a double play when she was playing second base. She had an arm for sure. I noticed she didn't pitch though. I wondered if she had wanted to.

Despite a few good hits, we lost. I was trying to be more Zen about losing. My mom says that: *I'm trying to be more Zen.* It means calm. I think she learned about it at her yoga class. Coach Vij was less Zen. He wanted to us to stay in contention. Now that we'd lost one, we were under the gun.

"We're going to have to win the rest of our games to stay alive," said Coach Vij after the game. "Can we do it?"

"It seems technically possible, Coach!" shouted Oscar, pumping his fist.

"Let's try that again with a *Yes, we can, Coach!*"

"Yes, we can, Coach!" we all shouted, except for Kahlil, who was too busy hustling to get to an orthodontist appointment. His mom was waiting with the car running, pointing at her watch. Most of the Ravens scattered, off to unlock bikes or meet their parents in the parking lot.

Coach Vij closed up the batting cage and started packing away the team equipment. I collected the scattered baseballs. A.J. went back to the dugout for his glove.

"Thanks, Caspar. You're always a real help to the team," said Coach.

I smiled. I liked to help. I liked to be part of a team. I always had. Maybe it was because I had no brothers or sisters. I was restless when there was no baseball. Like I didn't know who I was or what to do.

"Not just with how you help," Coach said. "There's something different about you."

I frowned, wondering what he meant. Could he tell?

"You have a special gift," he continued.

I do? I thought. "Fast wrists," I said.

"That too." He laughed. "But I mean you have a way of seeing potential in people. You notice skills. You'd be a good coach."

I wasn't sure what to say. It was one of the best things anyone had ever said to me.

"Thank you."

Hank appeared, back from the concession. He held up two freezies, both blue flavor, whatever that was.

"This is a future-victory freezie," Hank said, giving one to me. Then he produced two more that had been tucked into his baseball belt, handing them to Coach Vij and A.J., reminding me of batons in a relay.

"Awesome!" said A.J.

"Um, thanks," said Coach Vij. I wondered which he was more worried about—the lack of nutrition or the fact that they'd been tucked into Hank's pants.

"Oosh, that was cold," said Hank, smiling broadly. "To Ravens!"

"To Ravens!" we agreed, clinking freezies.

"We may start sucking after today, so let's enjoy the moment," added Hank.

"Hank, positive thinking," said Coach Vij, tapping his Ravens cap as if all the answers were there. "We've worked hard. Don't count us out."

"Right, we're tough," said Hank. The words were less convincing coming from his blue-stained lips.

"Hank, do you wanna stay and do some extra batting practice?" I asked.

"I just locked up the batting cage," said Coach Vij, taking a small taste of his freezie.

"Oh rats," said Hank.

"I'll stay if you guys want to practice," said Coach.

"You'd better text Mom," warned A.J.

"She'll be packing up from your sister's game," said Coach. "I can stay for half an hour. Then we have to fly."

I was already digging in my bag for my helmet. While I waited to take some swings, I realized this is what I had dreamed of. Hanging out as a boy with my friends, playing ball. I knew someday my secret would get out, but I had waited so long for this that I just wanted to enjoy the moment. It was my turn.

Sixth Inning

Coach Vij asked if I had a preference about who played catcher when I pitched, and I thought of Hank right away. It turned out Hank was a natural trapper. He's got the knack. And style. He springs up and throws down his mask and stomps around like some sumo wrestler. Hank isn't a gifted batter, but the dude can catch, he can read a play, and he has a strong arm. The number of baseball games lost on overthrows and bad plays by catchers—don't get me started.

Hank was at my house, playing a Lego *Lord of the Rings* video game, and I found myself thinking about what a great catcher he'd become. It had even surprised me. I decided to tell him.

"Dude," I said, as his avatar tried to leap from a cave, "you've become an ace catcher, no doubts." For some reason we'd been tagging all our thoughts with *no doubts* lately.

"Thanks, dude," he said just as his avatar died in an explosion. "Son of a monkey!" he shouted.

Why did everyone in Redburn say that?

Ever notice how when you are desperate to get some sleep, you can't? The night before our second playoff game I lay awake looking at my clock and listening to J.R. snore. My parents had given up on insisting that he sleep downstairs in his proper dog bed. My bedroom carpet was coated in his hair, and my mom had declared my room a disaster area. She'd actually made a sign for the door with a piece of cardboard and a black marker. She thought she was funny. Another time, in Toronto, she'd made a sign for the hall that read *Footwear Sale*. Okay, so my dad and I had left cleats, snow boots, flip-flops and a few pairs of running shoes in the hall. She had a point.

I must have fallen asleep sometime after 1:12 AM, though, because the next thing I knew my mom marched in at seven, telling me to rise and shine because it was two hours to game time.

"Okay, okay," I said, throwing my elbow over my face. The morning sun was already strong. It was going to be a hot one. Redburn was having an unusually hot summer, the locals kept saying.

I didn't like to have to rush to a game, so my mom knew to get me up in plenty of time. She had a glass dish ready on the table for me with yogurt, blueberries and some almond granola.

"Thanks, Mom," I said, sitting down. My new baseball pants fit perfectly, snug but long in the leg. It was important to look right for baseball, I thought. I liked to start off every game with a clean uniform—before I trashed it by sliding or diving.

My dad walked into the kitchen, already in his game gear—tracksuit and Cubs cap. He had this Saturday off. He sometimes worked weekends—it depended on his schedule—but he wanted to see me pitch my first game.

"Ya want some coffee, ace?" my dad asked, cradling his mug like it was a baby.

"No, I'm good," I said. I made it through half the dish of yogurt. That was all I could manage given the butterflies playing Twister in my gut. Then I heard ringing.

"Phone!" I shouted, trying to distract my parents from my unfinished breakfast.

My dad answered and handed me the phone. "It's for you."

"Hello, is this Mister Amazing?"

"Yes, Nana, it's Caspar. How are you?"

"I'm hot. My fan is on the fritz, and it's already broiling here. But I wanted to wish you good luck today. Just keep it cool, okay, because calm is a pitcher's best friend. You can't let the outside noise get to you."

I nodded. *Steel and oak.*

"You there, sunshine?"

"Yes, Nana. I miss you."

"I miss you too, lovey. Who are you playing today?"

"The Belleford Bruins."

They were the team I'd hit the grand slam against. I hoped they weren't out to get me. It wasn't as if I had flipped my bat like Bautista.

"Well, I know you'll make me proud, because you always do."

"Thanks, Nana. I hope you come visit soon."

"Okay, 'bye. Play hard, but play fair, Caz Cadman," she said. "Love you. Let me know how it goes."

~ ~

Dear Matt,

How is life in Toronto? That is so cool that you made the Red Devils. I wish I was there to practice with you. I bet the team will win again this year.

I pitched my first game today for two innings. My friend, Hank, was the catcher, and we did okay— three up, three down in the fourth inning, and two hits in the fifth. We won 11 to 7, partly because Gus hit a two-run homer, so we get to face the Rockets in the semis.

I've attached a photo of me in my Ravens uniform in our new backyard.

Write me back.

Your friend,

Caz

When Matt and I used to send emails at home, I'd sometimes sign mine *Lightn4Eva*, after our house team, but that seemed wrong now that we didn't play together. Matt's emails were becoming less frequent, which made sense, because he was busy with baseball and day camps. Coach Vij said Redburn was thinking of setting up an all-star team in the coming year to compete with other teams in the SeaTac area. That would be cool. The more base-ball the better, I figured.

My mom stuck her head into the office, where I was parked at the computer.

"Hey, how's the arm?" she asked. It had been a bit sore after the game. But winning always helps soothe the aches and pains.

"It's okay," I said, rubbing the top of my shoulder. I was a right-handed pitcher. It was better to be a leftie—they were in high demand in the big leagues—but you couldn't help the way you were born.

"Not too much more screen time, okay?" my mom said. Parents were all berserk about screen time. I spent half my waking hours throwing a ball or running, a quarter of my time on a bike or skate-board, and another chunk of time walking J.R. I was going to be okay with some screen time. It was like she couldn't help herself though. She listened to a public radio station.

"I'm just writing to Matt," I said, a slight lie. I had already sent my note to Matt. Mom nodded and headed downstairs to the Dungeon, which is what she called our new laundry area, a dark corner off the rec room. Once she was out of sight I googled *girl who is a boy*. About three hundred million results popped up, including one from a newspaper called *The Guardian* with the headline *The teen trailblazer for transgender children: From the age of two, Jazz Jennings knew she was a girl born in a boy's body.*

There was a photo of Jazz Jennings. She sat in a chair, wearing a pink dress, a necklace, nail polish and a big smile. She lived in Florida, a place I hoped to visit to see the teams at spring training. It was too bad that Jazz could not have just been born a girl, and me a boy. That would have been so simple. I had felt like a boy for my whole life. I wouldn't change my mind. Miss Linda had told me that sometimes your physical anatomy doesn't match your identity and that there were other kids like me and other people like me. In the article, they called Jazz Jennings *transgender*, the same word Miss Linda used. Jazz Jennings looked happy. That's what I was thinking when I heard the microwave door slam in the kitchen. The smell of microwave popcorn wafted to the office, and my stomach grumbled. Lunch had been a few hours earlier.

"Caspar, want some popcorn?" my mom called.

She knows I love corn of all kinds—corn on the cob, candy corn, but popcorn most of all. She says even when I was little, eating from those toddler trays,

I would polish off my corn first. Some things don't change.

I heard her in the hall, so I quickly clicked the box to close the article. If I had been born a boy, already in the right body, would I still be me, Caspar Cadman? It was kind of a scary thought.

I found my mom settled on our deck steps with the bowl of popcorn next to her. It was like she had made the popcorn to lure me there. It had worked.

"How did you like pitching?" she asked, holding up the bowl to me. The summer air smelled sweet from the blossoming shrubs in our yard.

"I liked it," I said, taking a hardball-sized scoop of popcorn.

"You seem okay with the pressure. You handled it well."

"I guess. Hank's good at framing the pitches."

"You were in a tough spot when the ump wasn't calling strikes. You walked a few."

I nodded, agreeing. I was busy stuffing more popcorn in my face. My mom really could have been a sportscaster. She didn't play it much, but she loves baseball. She didn't get her love of the game from Grandpa and Grandpa Ames, that is for sure. We watched a green hummingbird vibrate in front of us, then flit away.

"You had two runners on, but you got out of it."

"I told myself to settle it down. Then I told myself to try harder."

She thought for a second, looking off at the garden trellis so I couldn't see her face. When she turned back, I noticed that her eyes shone with tears. But she was smiling like she'd won the 50/50 draw.

"That's my boy," she said.

Seventh Inning

Over the three days after the quarterfinals game, our neighbors suddenly seemed to take notice of me. They even knew I was a pitcher.

"Hey, Caspar, big game coming up. You play for the Ravens, right?" a neighbor asked one day. He shook his head, as if we were doomed to go up in flames like a video-game avatar. Then he went back to his weeding. Sometimes they asked if my family was going to cut down the cedar hedges that blocked their light.

The day of the semifinals I was sitting at the kitchen table, staring at the toast my mom had placed in front of me. I hadn't gone downstairs to the Dungeon yet to get my baseball pants from the drying rack, so I was just wearing my underwear and my Ravens jersey.

"Eat your toast, Caz, you can do it, put a little power to it, *gooo*, Caz!" said my mom, who sometimes gave orders as baseball cheers, thinking she was funny. She was as nervous as I was, and it made her chatter more. I usually got tomb quiet.

"It's a great day for baseball," she said, looking out the greenhouse kitchen window. I loved to play baseball any day, but that didn't stop the hamster wheel in my head from spinning on playoff days. There was no way I could eat.

"Where's Dad?" I asked, resisting her attempt to be cheerful. I stood up to go find my ball pants.

"Hey," said my dad, striding in, holding a takeout coffee. "What's this? Is it the No-Pants, No-Problem playoffs?"

"Dad—"

"You're just going to open a can of No-Pants on them?"

"Stop," I whined.

"I brought you a pre-playoff game present," he said.

"I just need pants," I said, preparing to go downstairs.

"You'd better need a hug from Nana, 'cause that what's you're getting." Nana Cadman barged into the kitchen, her arms outstretched. She wore a shiny peach blouse, which she promptly crushed against me while administering two lipsticky kisses, one on each cheek.

"Nana!" I said, hugging back. She smelled like cold cucumbers and pink flowers. J.R. appeared, thumping his silky tail and head-butting Nana for some attention.

"Why are you here?" I asked, letting her give me another squeeze.

"I came to see some baseball, of course. My favorite player got traded to a new team."

My mom got Nana a cup of coffee while my dad got her bag from the car. No—bags plural. Nana never traveled light. It was just not her style.

~◦~

The semifinals were at a big park that we'd only played at once before. It had a concession stand, an announcing booth and big banks of metal bleachers—which were already filling up. I felt better when I saw the other Ravens. Oscar, Kahlil, Gus, A.J. and Coach Vij were at the park when we arrived. They were extra early. I saw most of the Rockets on the other side of the field, already jogging in a group. They must have shown up extra, *extra* early.

Some guy was driving around on a lawn mower shaped like a tank. The grounds must require twenty-four/seven mowing in such a rainy climate. The heat wave had passed, and Redburn was back to merely warm, which was fine by me—it's hard to grip the ball if you're sweating a lot. I hung up my Red Devils bag and touched the lettering for good luck. *Cadman.*

Between our warm-up drills, Gus walked over to me. Everything about him was big. He had this mass of curls and wide brown eyes, and he was broad-shouldered and strong. The loudspeaker was playing the song "Centerfield" by John Fogerty to get the crowd fired up. *I'm ready to play.*

"*Put me in cold,*" Oscar sang along, slightly off-key.

The word is actually *coach*, not *cold*, but I had other things on my mind. I let it go.

"Caz, I'm really nervous," Gus blurted.

"Nerves are good—shows you care," I said, echoing Nana. I thought for a second. "Don't think about the people watching. Just think about *your* job on the field—and do it."

"Yeah," he said, his big chest expanding as he exhaled. "You're right."

"They are zeroes, we are heroes," piped in Oscar, who'd been eavesdropping.

"That's not quite it," I said, but then my dad called me over to hit a few. All dads and moms were on deck for the playoffs. Coach Mira was there too, tossing fly balls to a group of Ravens. It felt so nice, my dad throwing and me hitting the balls into the fence, that I almost wished we could forget the game. I loved the *tink* of a Wiffle ball hitting the metal fence while we warmed up. It meant something ahead. The *crack* of a game ball meant something happening.

I saw Kyle approach Coach Vij, who was warming up A.J. to pitch the first inning. Coach listened, nodded, then pulled a sheet of paper from his clipboard. We'd won the coin toss to be home team, so that was an advantage. Everyone seemed to think we needed it. I was tired of hearing how many championships the Rockets had won.

Then the announcer cut the music. Five minutes to game time. Coach called us all in, and out of the corner of my eye I saw Nana, Mom and Dad sitting side by side in the bleachers. Nana had binoculars, a padded seat back, and a Blue Jays cap on her head. She knew the drill and didn't wave or blow kisses or anything. I was getting my head in the game.

"What did that guy Kyle want?" I whispered to A.J.

"Batting lineup to take to the scoring booth," he said.

That made sense, I figured, since Kyle's dad helped with the scoring.

We all took a knee by the dugout. This time we did it right. My brain was churning with thoughts of the game ahead.

"You've all worked hard to get here," said Coach Vij. "Now I want you to go out there and challenge those Rockets. Be on them. Support your teammates. Talk to each other. Focus. We're not letting anything go without a fight, right?"

"Right, Coach!"

"Let's do our cheer and play some ball!"

"Ravens rule!" we shouted, raising our fists in the air.

Hank accidentally bumped Gus.

"Watch it!" Gus said, clearly anxious.

My own playoff jitters sent me to the bathroom. I heard footsteps behind me and thought it would be Jerome, who had a nervous bladder too. I always used the stall, and no one had ever asked me about it. These bathrooms looked new. The whole park had recently been given a makeover, Coach Vij said. The town had been fundraising for years. There were two bathrooms, side by side, but both had a boy icon in pants and a girl icon in a dress, a line between them. The signs read *Restroom*. They were for everybody.

"Hey, wait—which one are you using, Cas*par*?"

The footsteps behind me had been Kyle's. I hated how he said my name. Hank claimed Kyle just liked to stir things up—that he'd always been that way, even in kindergarten. A.J. said Kyle regularly teased him about his lunch at school, saying it was smelly. Great. Something else to look forward to in September.

"They're the same," I said, pushing on one of the doors. I couldn't miss the start. I closed the door behind me to end the conversation, but my hands were still shaking when I stood at the sink to turn on the tap. Pre-game nerves. I was pitching later in the game—lots of time to get jumpy.

When I opened the door again, Kyle was still standing there, dragging one cleat on the ground and making hatch marks.

"Have a good game, Kyle," I said, turning back to the home dugout.

"You too, Cassie," he said, still watching his own toe drag in the dirt.

I froze, arms at my sides. I opened my mouth to speak, but I couldn't. I looked over and saw my mom watching me. She gave a half wave for luck.

Nana was cleaning her sunglasses with a cloth. My dad had gone to the dugout, helping Coach by calling out the assigned positions for the Ravens. The umps stood at home plate, talking and waiting. They appeared to be teenagers, one girl and one boy, but they had special navy shirts with collars.

"That's not my name," I said, forcing myself to use a big voice, like an ump.

"Sure it is," he said. "I saw the fancy baseball bag you kept showing off, and so I looked up the Red Devils U-11 team. On the Internet. Did you have Internet in Canada?"

I waited, not breathing. Something in my rib cage hurt like I'd been smacked with a fastball. It wasn't really a question, so I didn't answer. The game. I had to get into the game. Kyle was like a piece of gum stuck on my brain instead of my shoe. I needed him out of my head.

"There was only one girl on that team. Cassie Cadman. There was a photo in the paper and everything. You're not a boy. You're a girl. And a liar."

I remembered the photo. It had run in the *Toronto Observer*. Nana Cadman had kept three copies.

I looked at Kyle. He had small eyes that were close together and a thin angular face like his father, Mr. Budworth. Kyle hardly ever smiled. He smirked.

He sometimes pumped his fist if he scored a run or to make fun of someone's error. Even then he didn't seem happy. I glanced over and saw that my nana had given up playing it cool. She was tapping her wristwatch in an exaggerated way. Game time.

"Caz, get the lead out!" she yelled.

A few people in the crowd turned to stare, first at her, then at me. What Kyle said was sort of true, and I was someone who liked to tell the truth. But Kyle was also mean just to be mean. I had never met anyone quite like him.

"Kyle, I have to go. It's game time."

Steel and oak.

"I'm ready to play," I said, louder than I needed to. I was telling myself. I broke into a run, my jellied legs carrying me to the dugout, not letting me down.

"Caz, I don't know what planet you teleported to in your search for a bathroom, but please get your behind to left field in short order."

"Yes, Coach," I said, but it came out shakily.

Coach Vij looked at me again.

"Cadman," he said, putting his face to mine. I could see how much A.J. looked like him. "Who's going to win?"

"We are, Coach!" I squeaked, then jogged to my place in the field.

"Oscar," Coach shouted. "Put your glove on the right way!"

"Play is to first, no outs!" yelled Jerome, who was shortstop.

The announcer called the first batter, number 11, Carl Daigle. A.J. threw the first pitch, *ball high*, and the game was on. A.J. used his curve ball to confuse the batters and held the Rockets for the first inning, allowing just one hit—a hopper to second. The runner was left stranded, and it was our turn to bat. I heard Coach Mira cheering as we jogged off the field. My knees felt a bit wobbly as I reached the dugout—but it was a good nervous. Like I was excited for the team.

Maybe we can actually win this thing, I thought.

And then everything went wrong.

Hank was our leadoff batter.

"Up next, number 8, Hank Ottenburg," read the announcer.

"Let's go, Hank the Tank!"

Hank looked around, surprised, trying to see the source. My nana could be embarrassing, but she meant well. *If I'm here, I cheer*, she always says.

Hank's helmet had slipped down a bit, and I worried that he couldn't see.

Strike!

"Hank, push back your helmet!" shouted Coach. "And step into the box!"

Hank did both and hit a line drive. Kyle, playing shortstop, just missed the ball, leaving it to the second baseman. He scooped it up and hucked the ball too hard, and Hank reached first—just barely. We were going to have to hit better than that to make it a ball game.

Oscar was next. The pitcher had him chasing junk, and Oscar was swatting the air with his bat like King Kong trying to grab airplanes.

You're a girl. And a liar.

No. Caz, get him out of your head.

Oscar somehow managed to get hit by a pitch while he was dancing around. The ball bounced off his leg, and now we had two runners on. But it was as if we'd forgotten everything Coach Vij had taught us. I felt as if Kyle was watching me—like *all* the Rockets were watching me. I walked out to get on deck.

Gus, batting third, swung at two pitches nowhere close to the zone and then hit a pop fly deep into center field. *Don't run, Hank. Wait to tag up.*

Hank ran. The ball was caught. Gus popped out, and Hank was tagged out at third. The third baseman triumphantly raised his glove in the air as if it held the Lion King. This was going to be a long game. Oscar was nervously watching a wasp zip around the base, so he'd stayed put on first, thank goodness. One on, two outs.

"Next up, it's number 3, Cassie Cadman!"

I stopped right in the middle of my practice swing. I heard someone gasp, maybe my dad. Out of the corner of my eye I saw my mom's hands fly to her mouth. The microphone gave off a snarl of feedback. A different voice came on.

"Sorry, folks, I think that must be wrong. It's number 3, Caspar Cadman."

I stepped away from the plate and took another practice swing. My hands were sweaty.

"Nice cut, Caz!" Nana Cadman. There was no mistaking her.

Then I heard a snatch of words from the field.

"A girl?"

"He's a girl?"

"Dude, what the what?"

Kyle, from his position as shortstop, was pointing right at me. Shortstops were supposed to call out the plays, not talk about the players. Kyle pointed at me again.

"He's a girl named Cassie." I think Kyle meant to shout, but his voice came out in a squeak like a rusty screen door.

"Ball's in!" shouted the catcher. No one seemed to know what was going on.

"Is he really a girl?" asked the second baseman. "Wait, why should I care?"

Then this figure came at us from the dugout. It was Coach Cronck, the guy with the big beard, kicking up dust as he charged onto the field. He was dressed all in navy—cap, baseball pants, jersey. His fists were balled up at his sides. I wondered why he was so angry. Was he angry at me? I stepped away from the plate, watching. The ump seemed to hold his breath too.

Caz, take a practice swing. Do it.

It was shaky, but I did it. Everyone was waiting. The crowd started booing. "Play ball!" someone yelled. Not Nana Cadman, for once.

Coach Cronck was hissing at Kyle and waving his arms, kind of like he was showing what a big fish he'd caught. And the fish was a sturgeon.

Then Coach Vij left our dugout to check out the situation. He shuffled toward third base, looking confused. The booing got louder.

"What's going on?" shouted Oscar from first base.

I don't know, I mouthed.

Coach Cronck started yelling then, and we could all hear him, even above the booing.

"No shenanigans on game day!" I heard him tell Kyle. "You've been warned. You're distracting your team. If Liam wasn't sick today you'd be out."

Then he turned to Coach Vij, who was standing off to the side by third base. "Sorry, Coach. I apologize for my shortstop."

Coach Cronck returned to the Rockets dugout. Coach Vij stayed near third to do some base coaching as needed.

"Ball's in!" shouted the catcher.

I stood at the plate, stunned by everything that had just happened. A pitch came at me. I swung. I missed.

"You got this, Caz!" My mom. But it wasn't a good swing. It wasn't a good pitch either. The pitcher had me chasing.

I let one fly past me.

Strike.

I swung.

Strike.

At least I went down swinging.

I left Oscar stranded on first, and that closed the inning. I lowered my head as I walked back to the dugout. I didn't want to see Coach, my mom, my dad or Nana. It took Oscar a second to realize what had happened.

"The inning's over, dummy," the Rockets first baseman told him.

Timeout

Coach Vij had never called a timeout in a game before, but we had never been in this situation. We had played badly for four innings and were close to having the mercy rule called on us. The score was 12 to 5 for the Rockets—in the fifth inning. Everyone had expected them to win. Perhaps they hadn't expected them to murder us and leave our carcasses scattered on the field for an eagle to feast on. A.J. and Patrick had pitched well, but our fielding had been a comedy of errors—except it wasn't funny. We bumbled grounders and served up hefty over-throws to the Rockets. They gorged on our mistakes. Gus got knocked on the head when he was trying to trap a fly ball, and at least half the Rockets on the bench laughed.

We were running out of time. Even Nana had gone quiet, which was chilling. The sun cowered behind the clouds, as if even it knew the game was a lost cause.

"There's still time," Coach Vij insisted as we huddled, kneeling in the dirt by the dugout. "You are all great kids, and you are usually great players too."

He paused and rubbed his eyes. "I don't know what's happening out there."

"They said something about Caz," said Jerome.

"Yeah, they did. But do we care what they say?"

"No!" said Oscar, as loudly as ever.

Coach turned to me. "Caz, are you okay to pitch? You're up for the fifth inning. We can sub in Jerome if you want."

"Coach, about what they said…" I began. I twisted the band of my hat, which I held in my hands.

"Caspar, you don't need to say anything. We all know who you are. We know *you*. Remind me, what's the first rule of Ravens baseball?"

"Have fun?" I suggested in a small voice.

"No, it's that Coach gets the biggest brownie after the game. *Of course* it's to have fun!"

Hank clapped his hands together. "I think we're getting brownies," he whispered.

Coach Vij wasn't finished. "Ravens, you are not playing well. You are not having fun. I want you to get out there and do both. Right now! Okay?"

"Yes, Coach!"

"All right then. Team cheer," said Coach.

"RAVENS RULE!"

I swear I could feel the eyeballs sticking to me as I walked up to the mound. Hank lay in the grass while Coach helped him into the catcher's gear. The announcers in the booth played a Bruce Springsteen song, the one about the days that pass you by. Some of the spectators had already left, declaring it game over for the Ravens.

I took my five practice throws, and Hank lobbed them back. After the pummeling we'd taken, it seemed amazing to me that my legs could still hold me up, that my arm could still throw. But they did. The Rockets fans, normally a chippy bunch, were mostly silent, as was customary at a funeral.

The first batter, well, I didn't even hear his name called. He was tall with red hair and copper freckles. I threw a curve ball that I thought was right down the line.

Ball.

I looked at Hank. He mouthed, *What?*

Deep breath. Focus. One pitch at a time.

I threw another strike, a sinker that dropped just within the strike zone. As a pitcher I didn't throw wicked hard, but I was precise—and I knew it. I waited to hear the ump say, *Strike!* but he didn't. Making matters worse, the batters were just standing there.

And so the red-haired boy walked, and Rocket number 14 after him.

"I know a great optometrist!" I heard someone yell right after the ump called ball four and pointed for number 16 to take his walk. Nana Cadman could only stay quiet so long.

Mound Visit

Coach Vij signaled to the ump and walked toward me on the mound. Hank sprang up and also trudged over, robot-like in his catcher's gear. He didn't like to miss anything.

"Look, Caz. You're throwing strikes. But you're painting the corners. The ump is calling all the low ones as balls. You're going to have to change your location. Get the pitches higher. Because these batters aren't chasing."

The bases were loaded, all with my walks. I felt my eyes begin to itch, and my lip trembled. Yep, I was going to cry. I never cried. Well, hardly ever. Once when I dumped a mug of soup on my lap. And also during that last Jays game I watched in Toronto. Okay, sometimes I cried.

"The strike zone is like, the size of a Skittle," said Hank, shaking his head.

I laughed, just one sharp bark. I felt myself breathe again.

"I think it might be half a Skittle," I said, warming the ball in my hand. Like it or not, I had to get back at it.

"*Ball's in!*"

I threw a fastball, high in the zone. That fastball was gonna get a nosebleed, it was so high.

Strike!

Then I threw another, high.

Strike!

Then I threw one right down the line. The batter still wasn't swinging. It was like he'd forgotten how.

Strike! The ump made the "out" pump.

That was my first strikeout.

The crowd started chattering again, awakened by this turn of events. The next batter stepped up to the plate, and I tried it again—another strikeout. The batter walked away slowly, looking confused. The Rockets had seemed ready to walk their way to victory.

The next batter up was one of the Rockets' pitchers. He was heavyset and low to the ground. He knew the ump was calling strikes. He had a beauty of a swing. We reached a full count. The ump was letting me paint the corners. I decided to try a slider, hoping it would travel down and away.

"Crush it, Andy!" someone yelled from the crowd. "Let's stick a fork in this thing."

Bases loaded, two outs. One strike could end the inning. One swing could be a grand slam. Kyle was on deck, but instead of taking practice swings, he was watching me. He might have thought I was watching him, too, but I was keeping an eye on number 16, who had sidestepped off first base, leading off to run the second the bat connected with the ball. I spun around and whipped the ball to Jerome on first base, who shot up his glove like he knew the answer in math class.

Out! A small roar erupted from the Ravens' side. Jerome looked as if he'd been blasted with a stun gun. Then he smiled. It was likely his first successful pick-off.

"C'mon, boys, let's hit the sticks," called Coach Vij.

Jerome, Patrick and Hank all slapped me on the back as I left the mound. I felt a tiny half smile crack my face, my first of the game. As I walked back I thought, I won't let them take baseball from me. I didn't even know who "them" was. I just knew I wouldn't.

I'm ready to play.

Put Me In, Coach

Jerome's successful pick-off at first base seemed to have invigorated him, as if he'd conquered a video game, slammed down a chocolate shake and been handed a new dirt bike, all in one go.

"It's our last inning and our last at bat," said Coach. "Let's make the most of this." As home team, we batted last, and the inning was open-ended. There was no run limit. Getting a base hit would be a good start. I blinked at the scoreboard, hoping it would change. Nope. Still 12–5 for the Rockets. Judging from the trash spread across the bleachers, the fans remaining had tried every food item at the concession, from cotton candy to corn dogs. They wanted some action or an ending.

"Just make contact, Jerome," said Coach, giving Jerome a pat on the shoulder as he headed to the plate.

The pitcher looked like he was six feet tall. I knew he wasn't really, but the dude was big. He had long brown hair to his shoulders, which seemed to be a pitcher thing these days. I wondered if they believed their long hair had power, like in that myth. This guy had a crazy-long windup and a funny kind of sidearm delivery.

"That's different," said Coach Vij. "Guys, watch the pitcher."

Jerome was so thrown by the guy's style that he let two strikes go by without even swinging.

"C'mon, Jerry!" I yelled. "TRY!"

Jerome turned and stared at me. Coach turned to stare at me too. I'd never shouted during games except for a small cheer or two.

"YOU HAVE TO TRY!" I shouted again. It seemed like my last chance. If we were going to fall, we had to at least go down swinging. It drove me nuts when someone struck out looking at a good pitch. "Give it a rip!"

Jerome nodded, his black helmet bobbing. He swung on the next pitch and made contact with a convincing crack. I saw Coach Cronck's head jerk a bit, surprised. The hit took Jerome all the way to second. A double.

Coach Vij sent us up to bat quickly after that, cycling through our order—probably not wanting to lose momentum. A.J. was next. He battled for a long at-bat, fouling off five times before earning a walk. I noticed Coach Cronck holding his head in his hands after that. I could guess what he wanted. He wanted this game done so the Rockets could sail on to the finals. He wanted to save his pitchers, rest their arms, go home and have a beer or whatever— then plot the Rockets' winning lineup for the finals.

"Two on, no outs," shouted the Rockets short-stop. Kyle was playing second. He'd quieted down, and I wondered what his coach had said to him.

Patrick, a solid pitcher and fielder, was not a great batter. I thought he was heading for a strikeout, but then he got hit hard with a pitch. He hopped to first and stood there, rubbing his ankle. Then he sat down on the base, rocking in pain. He was really hurt.

"Caz," asked Coach Vij, "can you run for Patrick?"

"Yes, Coach," I said, springing up from the bench. My voice sounded normal, steady. I sounded like me.

I jogged to first. Coach followed behind and helped Patrick back to the dugout. My mom was already there, waiting with an ice pack from the cooler she carried to every game. As Nana would say, it wasn't my mom's first rodeo.

As she made her way back to the bleachers, Mom gave me a thumbs-up.

"Any base! No outs!" shouted the shortstop. We were back to the top of the order.

"C'mon, Rockets! Strike 'em out! What the hell are you doing?" yelled someone in the crowd.

Then something unexpected happened. Hank hit a line drive that burned right down the left foul line and deep into the field. Coach Vij waved us to run. Coach Cronck seemed to think it would be called foul, but it was fair, and the infield was an eggbeater blur of Ravens running. Jerome scored, A.J. scored, and I made it to third. Hank rested on second, wobbling off the base, then back on.

The Rockets appeared stunned by this turn of events. Oscar was up next. The way he wriggled around seemed to rattle the pitcher.

"Caz," he said, turning to me, "Coach Mira brought brownies!"

I gave Oscar a thumbs-up and pointed to my eyes. *Focus.*

Strike three!

Oscar turned toward the dugout, but then the catcher bumbled the block, dropping the ball and losing it in the dirt over by the fence. Passed ball!

"Oscar! RUN!" I shouted at the same time as Coach Vij.

"Caz, GO!" Coach Vij pointed toward home. I jetted from third, kicking up the dust, but halfway there I saw the catcher find the ball. I'd be out for sure. I did a U-turn and sprinted back to third.

"Slide!" yelled Coach.

I did, hearing a rip slice into my new baseball pants. Then, while I was down, I felt a fireball hit me in the shoulder. I lay on the ground in the dirt, hot tears squeezing out of my eyes. It felt like I had been shot with a rifle or even a flamethrower. My stomach lurched, and I thought I would vomit, the pain was so intense.

The third baseman cleared out of the way, and then Coach Vij and Coach Cronck were there, kneeling beside me. I still couldn't figure out what had happened. I wanted to get up, but I couldn't. My shoulder was blazing.

"Caz," said Coach Vij. "Where were you hit?"

"Shoulder," I gasped.

Coach Vij exhaled. Shoulder was better than head, even with a helmet. Coach Cronck held up some fingers, and I must have answered correctly, because he exhaled too. I pictured my mom, her fingers hooked over the wire fence, clinging there, waiting.

I didn't think anything was broken. A bone bruise, maybe. I'd had one before. They hurt.

"I'm okay," I said. The wave of shock passed. Coach Vij helped me to my feet. I wobbled a bit. The crowd clapped, even the Rockets fans, because you had to when a kid got up. Coach Cronck went to talk to the ump and then returned to third.

"Ump says you're out," Coach Cronck said.

"What? Your catcher drilled him!" Coach Vij said.

"Not on purpose," Coach Cronck said. The two men stood face-to-face, ballcaps nearly touching.

"Caz had already made the slide!" Coach Vij said, nearly shouting. "He was safe."

"Ump says the third baseman made the tag."

"Yeah, after the catcher disabled my player, and well after the slide."

"BOOOOO!" I heard. Great. Nana Cadman was going to get herself thrown out. Again.

"I'm challenging the call," said Coach Vij.

But it stood. I had beaten the tag, but nobody got a good look at my slide, because everyone was distracted by Oscar. I was out, according to the ump. And the ump is the boss.

Are you okay? my mom mouthed to me as I staggered to the dugout. I nodded, head down, so she couldn't see that I had cried. Another ice pack got passed along to me.

"One out, play's to first!" the shortstop called. He really was short and had a high, chippy voice that was beginning to bug me. I was mad. I did not like to play angry—but I would. The score was 12–7.

"*Ball's in!*"

Gus was up, and I was never so glad to see his wide, friendly face. He glared at the pitcher, stomping the dirt like a bull in baseball cleats. Even his curls looked angry.

Ball.

Hank was still fidgeting on second, leading off a couple of feet. The pitcher decided Hank was about to steal, but the third baseman wasn't paying attention. The pitcher's throw to try and catch Hank stealing landed deep into center field.

"*GOOOOO!*" the Ravens in the dugout yelled.

Hank took third, and Oscar took second.

"You morons!" shouted Kyle from his position in right field. The Rockets were turning on each other now.

Then Gus swung at a fastball, and by the crack, I could tell it was going deep. Kyle ran for it, but it bounced off the fence and shot back to center field. I laughed as Gus pedaled his sturdy legs around the bases. I was happy. Hank scored, Oscar scored, and Gus made it home to beat the tag. Now it was 12–10, with one out.

"Caspar, are you sure you're okay to bat?"

I nodded at Coach Vij.

The long-haired pitcher seemed twitchy now, shaking his hair from his shoulders.

Ball, ball, ball.

I would wait for my pitch. I'd been playing baseball since I was five years old. I could wait. I had known there was something different about me even then. I was the Joe DiMaggio of waiting.

Strike.

No, that wasn't the one. I saw Coach Vij pacing in a circle. Nana Cadman had her hands clasped in front of her. My dad and mom were sitting side by side, staring at home plate.

Strike.

A hush fell over the crowd as if an avalanche had fallen down, silencing us all with snow. Full count. This was the last inning and a big out, and everyone knew it. I didn't want to walk. Not today.

A high, hanging slider.

Crack!

The ball went soaring to left field and then just popped over the fence, like a diver arcing into a pool.

Moonshot.

I ran, my shoulder thumping with pain, my cleats touching every bag. I watched my own feet running. I heard my nana shouting, my mother.

"That is no girl!" I heard one of the Rockets say.

"Back-to-back jacks!" hollered Hank, pumping his arm wildly. He looked like he'd just been at an espresso bar with free samples. Man, he was happy.

As I rounded toward home, alone, I heard my whole team chanting my name. *Caz. Caz. Caz.*

∼

Three at-bats later, it was A.J. who hit a single to drive in the winning run. The Rockets left the field, dragging their feet, looking shocked. Kyle had a special message for me as the teams lined up to shake hands.

"You still suck, Cadman."

"Good game, Kyle," I said. "There's always next year."

For his RBI, A.J. was honored with first pick from his mom's tub of brownies. Coach Mira refused to let us dump Gatorade on him because his pants were new too. We listened. No one really wanted to annoy Coach Mira or waste Gatorade anyway. We hadn't used the Stingray yet. That was the great thing about baseball. There was always another game.

My mom and dad and Nana packed up the car while I hung out with the Ravens. We stretched out on a grassy hill next to the ball diamond. Coach Mira let us all have two brownies each, which we inhaled. We were already covered in grass stains and dust and now chocolate. My mother marched over and handed me a floppy blue ice pack.

"Good game, Caz," she whispered, then headed back to the car.

I think none of us could quite believe we'd done it, including Coach Vij. *Especially* Coach Vij.

"I knew we could do it," said Hank, his mouth full of brownie.

"The ump's call was wrong—you weren't out," Coach Vij said to me, not mad but thoughtful.

He was a guy who thought a lot, it seemed to me. "But we did the only thing we could do."

"Just keep playing," I said, brushing a crumb off my pants. I was going to hear about the tear in the knee later.

The greatest thing about winning was that we didn't have to listen to the Rockets doing their dumb cheer. I placed the ice pack on the grass and then leaned back, resting my shoulder on it. I stared up at the clouds while Hank the sportscaster replayed the game highlights.

Rockets can fly, I thought, but Ravens can too.

Eighth Inning

I spent the next four days going to practice and visiting with Nana Cadman, who was flying home just before finals. We all piled into the car to drive her to the airport. We'd moved so quickly from Toronto that we'd paid some company to drive our car all the way from Ontario to Washington. I was kind of jealous of our car, getting to see all those places. I mean, I guess the person driving got numb bum and was maybe a little lonely and bored, but I still thought driving coast to coast would be exciting. I wanted to do it someday. Once we got to the airport, I realized how much I didn't want Nana to leave.

"I am so proud of you, Caspar. I am so proud to be your nana. You're my diamond," she said, hugging me goodbye. She held me so close I could barely breathe.

I just nodded, my eyes filling with tears.

The next day the Ravens met at the same big ballpark to face the Kinsburg Knights. We went to extra innings, but the Knights were better than us that day. I'd hoped we'd take the crown. But we'd done better than everyone expected. Way better. When we got our silver medals, Hank shook his fist in the air and made a sound like Chewbacca when he got the medallion for helping the Rebels. Everyone laughed, even though some of us were trying not to cry.

I cried on the car ride home. I admit it. My mom insisted on trying to cheer me up. She knew I didn't like to lose. In fact, I had to battle my bad self—I pictured him sitting on my shoulder—to not be a sore loser.

"It gives you something to look forward to next year," my mom pointed out, turning around to face me.

"You're just trying to be positive, Mom!" I said, hugging myself. I knew my face was blotchy and red like a little kid's, but I didn't care.

My parents exchanged a look. They'd been through these losses with me before. I admit it:

I could get sulky when I lost. When we got home, I hugged J.R., wrote an email to Matt and checked baseball scores online. The Jays had won and the Mariners had won too, so that made me feel a little better. It was always good when your teams were winning. I had started to root for the Seattle Mariners—just a little.

My mom came into the office, holding the phone.

"It's for you. It's Hank. He wants to know if you want to go skateboarding."

"Tell him yes," I said.

"I think you can do that yourself," said my mom, handing me the phone.

Clearly the post-loss coddling was over.

Hank and I met at the park. It was the same one where he'd tried to show off his batting skills with a baguette. A lot had changed. He could definitely get a hit with the bread now.

"Caz," he said, sitting down on his skateboard, "are you really a girl?"

He was wearing a T-shirt that read *Caution: Full of Awesome.*

What really made you a girl? I didn't feel like a girl. I didn't want to be a girl. I did not think I was a girl.

"No," I said. "But everyone thought I was. It was a mistake. It made me kinda miserable."

Hank thought about that for a second. I was really worried he was going to ask about my *equipment*.

"I used to be allergic to hazelnuts," he said, standing up. "But I outgrew it. But I still don't like them."

He did a couple of moves on his board, slaloming from side to side.

"What would be your favorite walk-up song?" he asked, squinting in the sun under his helmet.

I'd thought about this before but couldn't make up my mind. The personal music played before you batted had to show you meant business and also get the crowd amped up. Get *you* amped up.

"Wow, Hank, that's a tough one. I'll need more time on that." I got on my board and tried to practice tic-tacs—quick little twists back and forth.

"Caz, I'm glad you moved here."

I thought for a second. "I am too," I said.

"You want to try skateboarding down the slide?" Hank asked, pointing to the playground.

Why not? It was the off-season now. We could take a few risks.

The next week, with baseball in hibernation until Fall Ball began, my parents decided I needed some "structure," so they put me in a day camp. One of the Westlake Jets players was in it, the girl Brooke—and guess what? She was nice. In fact, she was pretty cool. She really knew her baseball. I liked her so much that I was tempted to tell her about the Stingray—but I didn't. She went to Redburn Elementary, just like I would be. I was counting down the days. I was still dreading it.

I would be at Redburn Elementary for one whole year before moving on to middle school. It might be the longest year of my life. I was getting used to being summer-grubby in my board shorts and baseball shirts. But school was coming, ready or not. My parents had booked an appointment with my new counselor, who was named Mr. Miles. We would meet him just before classes started.

In Toronto, late August was the sweltering season. In Washington State, summer was cooling down, sort of like barbecue coals after a big cookout. My mom and dad took me for a walk to show me my new school. It was one of those not-optional outings. We'd driven past it before, but I hadn't really seen it close up. J.R. came along on the walk too, stopping to sniff every second shrub. My dad made jittery talk about our Redburn neighbors and the Jays' chances in September.

"Dad," I said. "Why do you wear that Cubs cap all the time? You aren't from Chicago."

"Do you really want to know?" he asked.

I nodded.

"I like the Cs. They're your initials. C.C."

"Don't make your dad cry now," said my mom.

I smiled. I had to admit, the school was nice. It had big playing fields, a tetherball post and an epic new basketball court. I could only hope that Kyle would leave me alone. But I knew I had friends now. I had teammates. They would stick up for me, and I would stick up for them.

When we got home, my mom checked messages in the hallway, as she always did. I think she hoped there would be something from her parents, saying they would come and visit soon. Mom said they still loved us but needed more time. Sometimes I forgot that Mom had left all her friends behind in Toronto too—Matt's mom and her friends from work. She must miss them sometimes.

I was hungry, as usual. Starving, actually. I started throwing open the cupboards, trying to find something to eat. My mom came into the kitchen, looking surprised. I worried something had happened to Nana Cadman or to Grandma and Grandpa Ames.

"What's up, Mom?"

"Caspar," she said. "You won."

"Won what?" I asked, still thinking of my dream snack. I was wishing for Pop-Tarts. But there was no way we had those. My mom mostly bought healthy non-processed food.

"You won that contest to go see the Mariners play. You get to take ten friends with you to the game. Remember?"

My brain flashed back to Hardy's Sports World and the clerk who used to be a Rocket. I remembered. It seemed like a long time ago.

"Awesome!" I said, doing an arm pump like I was starting up a chainsaw. My dad looked super excited, like this was *his* dream come true.

"Wait," I said. "Do I even have ten friends here?"

"I think you do, Caspar." My mom.

"I'll invite the whole team. All the Ravens."

"I thought you would." My dad.

Ninth Inning

Most of the Ravens accepted my invitation to go see the Mariners take on the Oakland A's. My mom even said she would smuggle in a tofu hot dog for Oscar if they didn't have vegetarian options. Coach Vij, Coach Mira and A.J.'s little sister, Anita, came along as well. Anita was decked out in full Mariners gear and knew all about the players, including their batting averages.

"Did you teach her all that, Coach Mira?" I asked.

"You bet, Caz. And you can just call me Mira now," she said.

My mom and Mira seemed to really get along, drinking coffees the size of fire hydrants and rolling their eyes about the same things their husbands and kids did. Dwight and Kahlil had said they couldn't come, and I didn't know why. Maybe it was because of what Kyle had said, but nobody trusted him. Almost everyone on the team had been one of Kyle's victims at some point. Maybe one day I would tell the rest of my friends—in my own words and in my own way, like I had with Hank. That night I just wanted to enjoy some baseball. I think Coach Vij already understood the situation. It was something about the way he said, *We* know *you.*

We'd been through a lot, us Ravens, and being in that stadium together was the best. We all wore our uniforms, and after the game we would get to run the bases together. I was already planning my email to Matt. He was pretty happy these days too, since the Red Devils had won the summer championships (like I'd predicted) for the second year in a row.

I'd only ever seen a ball game in Toronto, but most things here at Safeco Field were sort of the same. Whenever the Mariners pitcher got two strikes on one of the Oakland batters, the screen flashed *MAKE SOME NOISE!* to the crowd. Yelling was one of the best parts of a ball game. And the big buckets of popcorn, of course.

One time during a pitching change, the cameras turned our way, and we saw ourselves on the jumbotron. Oscar busted out his dance moves as if he'd been waiting all his ten years for that moment. I had never seen him dance that way, fluid like a water snake, and arm moves like he was shooting an arrow with a bow. I laughed so hard I thought I would snort Sprite out my nose. The rest of us threw our arms around each other, making the number-one sign with our fingers.

"This is the best thing," said Mira to my mom as the game resumed and we heard the crack of a bat. "This is summer."

This *is* the best thing—this is summer with friends, I thought. When the Mariners slammed a towering two-run homer in the ninth inning we all soared to our feet at once. I shouted, not even sure what I was saying because my words were blending with the roar of the crowd. That is the very best feeling, I thought, when your team causes you to jump for joy. You forget your troubles just for that one moment of amazement. I slapped high fives with all my new friends and even some people behind me that I didn't know. And for that one moment I felt like the luckiest boy on earth.

Acknowledgments

Full confession: I've never hit a grand slam or a home run. I've never thrown a perfect slider. Or even a so-so slider. Although I grew up in Toronto—including during the era that the Toronto Blue Jays won two World Series—I did not really get baseball. Then I had kids. And those kids loved baseball. Since then, I have spent hundreds of hours at ballparks, counting pitches or running the scoreboard—but mostly just watching and cheering. Being at all these games led me to become a true baseball fan, and some of the players I observed at the diamond inspired me to imagine Caz Cadman.

I'm a cisgender person, which means the gender I was assigned at birth fits how I feel. To help me better understand Caz, I read books, articles and blogs, including *Some Assembly Required: The Not-So-Secret Life of a Transgender Teen* by Arin Andrews, and the warm and wonderful middle-reader book *George* by Alex Gino. I also listened to many episodes of the captivating podcast "How to Be a Girl: Daily Life with My Transgender Daughter" by Marlo Mack, which you can find here: http://www.howtobeagirlpodcast.com.

I sincerely thank the early readers of this book, particularly the transgender boy and his family who weighed in on what worked and what didn't ring true. I am grateful for their insights, observations, and astute suggestions. This family also suggested several resources to share, including **Gender Spectrum:** https://www.genderspectrum.org/ and **Trans Care BC** http://transhealth.phsa.ca/trans-101, which includes a page of terms and information that is helpful no matter where you live. Any trans people who need immediate support can contact the **Trans Lifeline:** https://www.translifeline.org/ in Canada or the U.S.

My appreciation also goes out to Dr. Aaron Devor, Chair in Transgender Studies (http://uvic.ca/transchair) at the University of Victoria, who was kind enough to review the manuscript. The university is home to the world-leading Transgender Archives, and you can learn about them here: http://transgenderarchives.ca.

My good friends Andrew and Suzanne MacLeod read an early version of this story and offered warm encouragement when I needed it. Thanks as well to my employers for allowing me to go on leave to work on books. I wrote a draft of this book during those five months.

In 2016, to my disbelief, I won a national contest in which the prize was a trip to see the Toronto Blue Jays play a series against the Seattle Mariners at Safeco Field. It was a magical experience—and helped me write this book. Thank you to the Toronto Blue Jays.

My gratitude to all the volunteer coaches and dedicated parents who make the game happen, especially everyone at the Carnarvon Baseball Club. And a fist bump to the 2017 Mosquito AAA Black Eagles coaches, players, and parents. We took a lot of ferries together, my friends.

A round of high fives to the stellar team at Orca Book Publishers, including Andrew Wooldridge, Jen Cameron, Vivian Sinclair, Teresa Bubela and my wise editor, Tanya Trafford. Thank you for believing in this book.

A bat flip to my incredible agent, Kerry Sparks of Levine, Greenberg, Rostan Literary Agency, who would always be a first draft pick for my team.

My love goes out to my relatives in Fredericton, New Brunswick—the McMullen, Phillips and

Skulsky families. Thank you for hosting my children for a week during the summer of 2017. They had the time of their lives while I revised this manuscript. My father, Ron Manzer, is the kindest, gentlest person I know. Thank you for everything. Thank you, too, to Barrie and Marjorie Leach, and to my niece, Charlotte—for being such a devoted reader!

I would also like to acknowledge the memory of my mother, Kathryn Helen Manzer, who valued her signed baseball from Carl Yastrzemski. Even my spellcheck knows his name! I also dedicate this book to my sister, Patricia Kathryn Manzer, who sat in the stands at a lot of rainy baseball games. She left us far too soon, and we will remember her every day.

This book would not have happened without the love and support of my own ball club: my son, A.J., my daughter, Briar, and my husband, Coach David, who always encourages batters to "put a little dance in your stance."

And, in the final inning, I want to thank all the kids like Caz, and the parents, activists, educators, librarians, health-care providers, writers, friends, relatives, teammates, and coaches, who are out there, every day, working to make the world a better place for all children.

JENNY MANZER is the author of the young adult novel *Save Me, Kurt Cobain*. She lives in Victoria, British Columbia, with her family. Follow her on Twitter @jennymanzer or find her at jennymanzer.com.